Meet Samantha Holt . . .

Murder never happens to ordinary people. Gangsters, loan sharks, drug dealers certainly. Politicians maybe. It never involves anyone you know, like the guy who owns the dry cleaner's down the street or the mechanic who works on your car. Or your veterinarian. And it's hard to imagine any place less attractive to the criminal element than Brightwater Beach, Florida, where the median age is twenty years above the national average, and line dancing is a popular pastime.

At least that's what I thought . . .

MORE MYSTERIES FROM THE BERKLEY PUBLISHING GROUP . . .

JENNY McKAY MYSTERIES: This TV reporter finds out where, when, why . . . *and* whodunit. "A more streetwise version of television's 'Murphy Brown.'" —*Booklist*

by Dick Belsky
BROADCAST CLUES
THE MOURNING SHOW
LIVE FROM NEW YORK

CAT CALIBAN MYSTERIES: She was married for thirty-eight years. Raised three kids. Compared to that, tracking down killers is easy . . .

by D. B. Borton
ONE FOR THE MONEY
THREE IS A CROWD
TWO POINTS FOR MURDER

KATE JASPER MYSTERIES: Even in sunny California, there are cold-blooded killers . . . "This series is a treasure!" —Carolyn G. Hart

by Jaqueline Girdner
ADJUSTED TO DEATH
THE LAST RESORT
TEA-TOTALLY DEAD
MURDER MOST MELLOW
FAT-FREE AND FATAL

FREDDIE O'NEAL, P.I., MYSTERIES: You can bet that this appealing Reno P.I. will get her man . . . "A winner." —Linda Grant

by Catherine Dain
LAY IT ON THE LINE
WALK A CROOKED MILE
SING A SONG OF DEATH
LAMENT FOR A DEAD COWBOY

CALEY BURKE, P.I., MYSTERIES: This California private investigator has a brand-new license, a gun in her purse, and a knack for solving even the trickiest cases!

by Bridget McKenna
MURDER BEACH
DEAD AHEAD

CHINA BAYLES MYSTERIES: She left the big city to run an herb shop in Pecan Springs, Texas. But murder can happen anywhere . . . "A wonderful character!" —*Mostly Murder*

by Susan Wittig Albert
THYME OF DEATH
WITCHES' BANE

LIZ WAREHAM MYSTERIES: In the world of public relations, crime can be a real career-killer . . . "Readers will enjoy feisty Liz!" —*Publishers Weekly*

by Carol Brennan
HEADHUNT
FULL COMMISSION

KAREN ANN WILSON

EIGHT DOGS FLYING

A Berkley Prime Crime Book / published by arrangement with the author

PRINTING HISTORY
Berkley Prime Crime edition / December 1994

ISBN: 0-425-14490-9

Berkley Prime Crime Books are published by
The Berkley Publishing Group,
200 Madison Avenue, New York, NY 10016.

PRINTED IN THE UNITED STATES OF AMERICA

10 9 8 7 6 5 4 3 2 1

In memory of Samantha, 1985–1993

ACKNOWLEDGMENTS

•

I wish to acknowledge the technical assistance of the following people: Paul and Sue Capal, Capabal Kennels, Tarpon Springs; Joe Kunz, USDA, St. Petersburg; Detective Richard Howard, Clearwater Police Department; Michael Schroeder, DVM, Animal Hospital of Treasure Island. Any errors, manipulations, or omissions of fact are entirely my own.

I would also like to thank Bonnie Goldman and my father, Donald F. Wilson, for reading my drafts and for making so many useful suggestions, most of which I heeded.

Special thanks go to my agent, Robin Rue, and my editor, Ginjer Buchanan, for their encouragement and hand-holding during the publication of this, my first novel.

Most of all, I would like to thank my husband, Robert A. Knight, for his constant support in whatever I do.

PROLOGUE

•

Murder never happens to ordinary people. Gangsters, loan sharks, drug dealers certainly. Politicians maybe. It never involves anyone you know, like the guy who owns the dry cleaner's down the street or the mechanic who works on your car. Or your veterinarian. And it's hard to imagine any place less attractive to the criminal element than Brightwater Beach, Florida, where the median age is twenty years above the national average, and line dancing is a popular pastime. At least that's what I thought.

When I came to Florida, all I wanted was a little peace and quiet and a chance to start over, having mucked up my first shot at life so thoroughly. I chose Brightwater Beach, because my aunt Grace lived here for a short while and thought it was the greatest thing since Medicare. She and Uncle Randy played bridge every Monday, Wednesday, and Friday, and on Sunday they ate the early-bird special at the Hungry Fisherman. Until Randy died. Then Grace went back to Connecticut. There aren't a lot of single men in Brightwater Beach. I guess that's another reason I chose it.

I live in Paradise Cay, a suburb of Brightwater Beach. It is composed entirely of dredged-up bay bottom, having preceded the Department of Environmental Regulation and the Clean Water Act by several years. From the air, it looks like a giant comb, each tooth representing a small fortune to some clever New York developer with a good adman.

Most of the residents in Paradise Cay are retired, well-off, and own pets, a fact that did not escape my boss, Louis Augustin, DVM, when he was looking for a place to set up shop. Our clientele also includes a few less fortunate, but no less conscientious, pet owners. This has resulted in a somewhat flexible fee schedule. However, it's preferable to having a kennel full of feline and canine inmates held hostage by unpaid bills. Fortunately, no one has complained. Few of our female clients would, mind you. Even when Dr. Augustin wears his grubbiest jeans, perfectly sensible women are falling all over themselves to bring their poodles and Persians to him, as if he were the only vet in town. Chippendale's couldn't pack them in any better.

Of course, they don't have to put up with him day in and day out. Working for Dr. Augustin is like going to a potluck supper. Some dishes are pretty good. Some are not so good. Sometimes you wish you'd stayed home. I suppose most any job has its good days and its bad days. However, with most jobs you can usually see the bad days coming. You'd need tea leaves or chicken entrails to see what a day at Paradise Cay Animal Hospital was going to be like. Dr. Augustin is a little schizoid at times. I like to think it has to do with the phase of the moon, but it's probably all the sugar and preservatives he eats.

And every week, Dr. Augustin is on some new crusade or other that rarely has anything to do with veterinary medicine. Even though he's forty years old, he apparently hasn't decided what he wants to be when he grows up. As a result, he dabbles, writing numerous letters to the editor and attending City Commission meetings, where, in his allotted three minutes, he preaches social change with the fervor of a TV evangelist. Most of the time the commission goes along with him, or they table the matter in the hopes that the following meeting, Dr. Augustin will be home delivering puppies or something.

In the few instances where some special-interest group wins out, there's hell to pay back in Paradise. I once hung a sign up in Dr. Augustin's office that read: WE COMFORT THE TROUBLED AND TROUBLE THE COMFORTABLE. I tore it down after he told me if being comfortable meant getting a paycheck, I must be right. He was smiling, but I didn't want to take any chances.

Just when I think I can't handle the stress another minute, he goes and wrests some cat or dog from the jaws of death or lets some little old lady skip without paying her bill, and I decide to tough it out awhile longer.

Lately, there's been some talk of him running for a seat on the City Commission. *He* hasn't said anything, but if Clint Eastwood can get elected mayor of Carmel, Dr. Augustin should be able to get elected to the Brightwater Beach City Commission. Dirty Harry has nothing over Louis Augustin when it comes to entertainment value.

As I see it, the only real drawback to his habit of taking on outside projects is that Dr. Augustin expects his employees to take them on as well. Whether we want to or not. Until recently, however, we'd never been involved in anything especially noteworthy or dangerous. It had never occurred to any of us that working for a veterinarian could get us much more than flea-bitten. After all, doctoring cats and dogs isn't supposed to be glamorous or filled with intrigue. It certainly isn't supposed to involve murder.

Of course . . . that was before we got involved with Dr. Augustin's ex-wife, Rachel, whose normally placid greyhounds suddenly were trying to kill people. It was also before Dr. Augustin decided he wanted to be Nero Wolf when he grew up.

CHAPTER 1

•

Saturday, February 5

For the second day in a row, I overslept. It was nearly eight when I finally got to the clinic. Carl Meyerson was waiting for me by the front door cradling a medium-sized cardboard box that read TY-D-BOL TOILET CLEANER on the side. His seven-year-old daughter, Jessica, was with him. She alternately clutched at his pantleg and sobbed, a high-pitched, hiccuping sound that made me instantly wary. I climbed out of my car and approached them.

Mr. Meyerson's shirt and arms looked like a Jackson Pollock mural, as if someone had deliberately flicked red paint all over them. I could feel my palms start to sweat, and for one brief moment I thought about getting back in my car. But the box was drawing me to it like a magnet.

"We were walking Missy down to the park, Miss Holt, just like we do every Saturday morning," Mr. Meyerson began, almost convulsively, "and this tall, skinny, tan dog—you know, one of those racing dogs—came out of absolutely nowhere and grabbed Missy by the neck and started shaking her back and forth." He paused long enough to draw a breath, then plunged ahead. "By the time we got Missy away from the dog, a woman—I guess the owner—was there, screaming, like she was afraid of him, and then a man came up and took hold of the dog, saying they had just picked him up from a racing kennel, and they were really sorry and would pay for everything."

I peered in the box. The little Yorkshire terrier was breathing, albeit rapidly, and she was conscious. Blood covered her, head to tail. Her skin lay back from her neck and shoulders in thin, irregular strips. She looked like a ripe, red, freshly peeled plum. I could see a piece of bone sticking out of one of her rear legs. I turned to the front door, quickly unlocked it, and ushered Meyerson and his daughter in. Almost immediately a muted chorus of barking began back in the kennel. The room smelled faintly of disinfectant and wet dog.

I put my purse on the reception desk. "Let me take Missy to surgery, Mr. Meyerson," I said, gently, surprised my throat could still produce sound. "Dr. Augustin should be here any minute."

Meyerson eagerly thrust the box in my direction. Jessica looked up at me with a mixture of relief and trust in her eyes. God, how I hate that look. Fortunately, Dr. Augustin came through the side door just then. He did a quick survey of the damage and looked over at Mr. Meyerson.

"Carl, why don't you and Jessica go on home? This will take a while. I'll give you a call the minute we're through."

Mr. Meyerson nodded. He took Jessica's hand, and without looking back, the two of them walked slowly across the room and out the door. An air of resignation trailed after them. Dr. Augustin didn't say anything. He switched on the AC, then led me and the Ty-D-Bol box down the hall.

"I thought greyhounds were quiet, gentle dogs," I said after a considerable length of time. I turned off the anesthesia machine.

"As a general rule, they are," Dr. Augustin said. "But you

know as well as I do, greyhounds are trained to chase things. Rabbits, cats . . . Yorkies. Anything small and quick. They don't do it out of meanness, Samantha."

He stripped off his surgical gloves and pitched them on the table. Then he took off his gown, wadded it up, and threw it angrily on top of the gloves. His thick, curly hair, damp with sweat, stuck to his forehead in black clumps, and tiny red dots of blood decorated his right cheek. He looked exhausted. I knew he wasn't happy about the way the surgery had gone. His silence usually meant somebody had screwed up. Since I was pretty sure it wasn't me, he had to be angry with himself. The dog would recover, and all of her bones would function like they were originally designed to, but somewhere along the way Dr. Augustin must have felt he'd performed less than brilliantly.

We could hear the noise in the reception room. It was well past ten o'clock, and the appointments were beginning to back up. Earlier, Cynthia Caswell, our receptionist, had peeked cautiously into the surgery and inquired about how much longer we would be. Dr. Augustin had growled, "Longer than we would if people didn't keep interrupting us." Cynthia had opened her mouth then closed it; wisely, I thought. She'd looked at me, her expression seeming to say, "If he were *my* child, I'd paddle his fanny, but good." Then she'd left, her navy wool-blend skirt snapping sharply behind her, like a whip. Now she was back, but this time she stood silently in the doorway, hands on hips, staring at us.

Cynthia reminds me of my mother. She is about the same age, has the same pleasingly plump shape, and right then, the same look on her face my mother used to get when I hadn't done my chores in a timely fashion.

Dr. Augustin apparently got the message. "I'm going to take a shower," he said. *"Five minutes!"* Then he left.

Cynthia looked victorious. She winked at me, thrust out her bosom until the buttons on her blouse threatened to disengage, and headed for the reception room.

Missy had begun to stir. I carried her to a recovery cage and reconnected her IV line. Then I got on the intercom.

"Frank, I need you in surgery, pronto!"

Frank Jennings, the clinic's kennel manager, is a drummer in the rock group Death something. I've never heard them play and never intend to, but one of our clients said they weren't too bad, if you like lots of noise and lyrics about blood and the afterlife. Frank certainly looks like a rock musician. He is twenty-eight, tall and gaunt, with long, straight brown hair and pasty white skin. He is always appropriately attired in blue jeans that could have been washed in battery acid, for all I know. The holes leave very little to the imagination.

For some strange reason, he has taken a liking to me, even though I am older then he is and heavier by at least twenty pounds. He is always trying to get me to go out with him. The thought of Frank touching me is like a cockroach running up my back. Never mind the fact that he is good with the animals, rarely complains, and keeps the clinic practically spotless. He has trouble getting to work on time, presumably because of his night job, but once there, he earns his keep. I'll have to give him that.

"You rang?" he said, coming into the room. His T-shirt was drenched, and he smelled like flea shampoo.

"Would you mind cleaning up this mess for me?" I asked, trying not to look at him. "Dr. Augustin and I are running behind. Just put the instruments in the sink, and I'll take care of them later. Thank you, Frank." I left before he could answer, feeling his eyes following me, trying to see through my lab coat.

• • •

Our first appointment was Bruiser Ames, a huge orange-and-white tomcat who was as affectionate as he was moth-eaten. Although the Ameses paid for Bruiser's annual vaccinations, they refused to have him neutered or keep him inside, so he continued to get into fights with every other intact male cat in town. Periodically, Mr. Ames alone or Mrs. Ames in the company of their five children would have to bring him in, because one of the bites had gotten infected. This time it was Mrs. Ames's turn, according to Cynthia.

I went out to the reception area. The place looked like a frontline first-aid station. Instead of cots and litters, cat carriers rested on chairs and on the floor, and several dogs growled and lunged at one another, their leashes secured to the desk and the magazine rack. The Ames children were scattered about, entertaining themselves sticking their fingers into the various carriers. I was amazed no one had been bitten yet.

"Frank is running behind on his baths today," Cynthia told me. She looked disgusted. I decided not to tell her he was cleaning up the surgery for me. I took the Ames file from her.

"Good morning," I said to Mrs. Ames. She was a young woman, around twenty-five or twenty-six, but had the figure and overall appearance of someone much older, owing probably to her long string of pregnancies and living with Mr. Ames. I was pretty sure she didn't really believe everything her husband advocated. But she was doing the wifely thing, supporting him in his various causes. I couldn't imagine her ever opposing him, in bed or otherwise.

She was dressed in a dark green, long-sleeve turtleneck and a burgundy corduroy jumper that was too tight across her ample chest. She kept pulling down on it, as if it might ride up over her head if she didn't. A blob of what appeared to be baby cereal clung like a leech to the left shoulder of the jumper, and one of the pockets was torn loose, probably by some tiny hand grasping for attention. Her long brown hair was gathered at the nape of her neck in a bun. She wore no makeup.

She'd always struck me as the kind of woman who grew her own tomatoes and green beans without any pesticides and bought her peanut butter at a health-food store. Unfortunately, she also apparently believed that children should be allowed to do whatever the "spirit" told them. The Ames children listened to some interesting spirits.

I picked up Bruiser's carrier and led Mrs. Ames and her clan into Room 1. Dr. Augustin was waiting for us, looking freshly scrubbed. He had changed into a pale blue, long-sleeve shirt that was too big everywhere except at the shoulders, and denim jeans that weren't too big anywhere. He rarely wore slacks. I'd only seen him wear a tie once, at his father's funeral. He and his father had never been close—separated, I supposed, by the length of their hair—but I presumed he had felt it necessary from a social standpoint to be formal on such an occasion. He'd worn his best jeans with the tie.

"Good morning, Mrs. Ames," he said. "Sorry to keep you waiting, but we had an emergency." He opened the carrier and extracted Bruiser, who immediately began to purr.

As usual, the three oldest children felt compelled to "help." I could tell by the set of his jaw that Dr. Augustin was trying to keep hold of his tongue. He worked quickly and efficiently on Bruiser, dispensing with his usual masculine charm, skipping the chitchat he reserved for his female clients.

As the Ames family was leaving, Dr. Augustin once again recited his litany about the benefits of neutering, and Mrs. Ames once again said that to deny Bruiser his "maleness" would be inhumane. The voice was Mrs. Ames's, but it was Mr. Ames talking.

"Good-bye and thank you, Dr. Augustin," Mrs. Ames said from the doorway. Dr. Augustin nodded and smiled, and a faint blush of pink colored his face. Then she began shepherding her brood toward the front desk, and Dr. Augustin went through the lab into his office.

Our next three appointments were for routine vaccinations and a chest X ray. We were finished by 1:30, an hour and a half behind schedule. That left just thirty minutes for lunch. I hadn't planned anything, only a sandwich from the corner deli, so I agreed to watch the front while Cynthia walked to the fabric store up the street. She promised to hurry.

At 1:45, Mrs. Glynnis Winter drove up in her Cadillac Seville. Through the plate-glass panel that served as the clinic's front wall, I watched her slide out of the car and close the door. Frosty, her Maltese, lay in the crook of her arm as always, like a great benign growth no one had seen fit to remove.

Mrs. Winter's auburn hair was perfectly coiffed. I imagined she wrapped her head in toilet paper each night or did whatever women who always look beauty-parlor perfect do to stay that way between visits. Her sleek, aerobicized body was encased, like some metamorphosing butterfly, in a slinky, translucent green jumpsuit. I had to admit, she looked sensational.

I needed to stretch, so I got up and opened the door for them. "Good afternoon, Mrs. Winter," I said, reaching out to scratch Frosty's head. The little dog's long, pink tongue was fully extended, and he was breathing like some doggie devil was after him.

"Good afternoon, Miss Holt. You said to come by anytime. . . ." She tucked her dog closer to her and breezed past me, trailing Obsession. Once at the reception desk, she added, "And he hasn't eaten a bite since last night, *per* your instructions." She planted a kiss on Frosty's nose. "Poor little baby is starving to death."

I glanced at the pristine, panting body, its forelock of hair held up by a dark green ribbon, and knew with absolute certainty that Frosty was not starving to death.

"Yes, Mrs. Winter," I said.

She was smiling at me, her perfect teeth blindingly white under the fluorescent fixtures. I wondered, briefly, who her dentist was, then decided I wouldn't be able to afford him.

I reached for her dog. "Come, little one, let's take a walk," I said. The animal strained toward Mrs. Winter, a look of intense horror in his eyes. Mrs. Winter responded by stepping away from me, as if I'd just eaten garlic, her precious puppy clutched to her breast.

"Perhaps I should go with you and hold him," she said.

I sighed inwardly, praying that Cynthia would walk in and take the woman off my hands.

"This will be quick, Mrs. Winter. Really. Most dogs are pretty easy to work with when their owners aren't around—that protective instinct, you know."

She and I both knew that Frosty wasn't interested in protecting anyone except himself. But I couldn't think of anything else that might pry loose the hairy tumor wrapped like a boa constrictor around her salon-tanned arm. I reached for her dog once again, and she reluctantly handed him over.

"You have a seat, and I'll be right back," I said. Frosty and I left her admiring her manicure.

I went into the lab.

Patricia Jane Thompson, Dr. Augustin's laboratory technician, was rinsing off her fork and spoon. She turned around. "Need some help?" she asked.

P.J., twenty, is a nice kid, hardworking and conscientious, but she lacks self-confidence and is scared half to death of Dr. Augustin. I feel a certain kindred attachment to her.

"We need a blood sample from Frosty, here. For a profile." I inclined my head toward the reception room. "Mrs. Winter is waiting."

"Sure," P. J. said. She took Frosty and followed me into the treatment room. "Isn't Mrs. Winter that rich old widow with the 'hots' for Dr. Augustin?"

I stared at her. "She's not that old, P.J."

"Sure. Okay. But she does seem to spend a lot of time here."

"True," I said. "Particularly since there's nothing wrong with her dog a decent dog food wouldn't cure."

"Maybe she's lonely," P.J. offered. "Or bored."

"Husband hunting is more like it," I said. I finished drawing my sample and transferred it to a collection tube, which I handed to P.J. Then I lifted Frosty from the table.

"She doesn't seem his type, somehow," P.J. said.

"No, not in the least." But, I thought, money is a powerful attractant.

After I'd returned Frosty to his owner, I went into the bathroom and closed the door. Staring at myself in the mirror, I realized that at thirty-something, I would never look as good as Mrs. Winter did at forty-something. My thick, blond hair, practically unmanageable under the best of circumstances, was even wilder that day because of the unseasonably humid weather we'd been having. And my eyes were too small. I pulled up on my lids in an effort to produce that wide-eyed look men supposedly find so attractive. I resembled one of those plastic medical models, where the eyeballs jut out from a skull devoid of skin. Lovely. I smoothed down the collar of my uniform, straightened my name tag, and opened the bathroom door.

Dr. Augustin was waiting for me. "Were you planning to spend the rest of the afternoon in there, Samantha?" he asked. "We have clients, you know."

I looked at my watch. It was 2:10. I'd only been in the bathroom for a minute or so. I gnashed my teeth. "Mrs. Winter popped in just before two with Frosty. I had to get a blood sample for that profile you wanted. I haven't even eaten lunch yet."

He didn't appear very sympathetic. "I know. I passed her on my way in. Did you get a load of that outfit?"

For a second his eyes glazed over, and he looked like a stray dog on the verge of starvation. Then he came around. He stared at me. "Well, what are you waiting for? Let's get cracking!" He took off down the hall toward the exam rooms.

Lunch was obviously out of the question. I shook my head and followed dutifully along after him, my crepe soles making mouse sounds on the linoleum.

The rest of the afternoon was uneventful. We stayed on schedule, which was a pleasant change from earlier, and locked up at a quarter past five. Dr. Augustin said he would come back in a couple of hours to check on Missy Meyerson and would leave me a note. We alternated coming in Sundays to medicate. That weekend it was my turn.

Later, as I drifted off to sleep, I saw a ghostly image of Mrs. Winter with Frosty glued to her arm running down the street, her slinky green jumpsuit and perfect hair splattered with blood. A huge greyhound was in hot pursuit, snapping and snarling at her heels.

CHAPTER 2

•

Monday, February 7

The morning started out like an ad for the local Chamber of Commerce, with a cloudless, deep azure sky and a temperature of fifty-five degrees. It had rained most of Sunday, and the air smelled like freshly washed, sun-dried laundry. Everything sparkled—the boat channel, the little, white, look-alike houses with the dolphins painted on their shutters. Even the gravel lawns looked inviting.

I got to the clinic at my usual time of 7:30 in good spirits. I'd run three miles in less than twenty-eight minutes, a personal best for me, and managed to avoid the doughnut shop. By the time everyone else arrived, I'd made coffee and started treatments.

Monday promised to be slow. Cynthia hadn't scheduled any surgeries, and there were still a few appointments open. I decided to get a head start on our food order. When the phone rang, I was in the supply closet behind Cynthia's desk.

"Oh no, that's just *terrible*!" I heard Cynthia say after a moment. "I hope she's going to be all right."

I stepped out of the closet, clipboard in hand.

"Yes, yes, I'll put you right through." She pressed the intercom button. "Dr. Augustin, John over at Animal Control is on line one. Right." She pressed another button and hung up. She looked at me, her face grave.

"Animal Control wants Dr. Augustin to examine and then euthanize a dog that attacked a little girl this morning," she told me. "The child is in surgery at St. Luke's. She might die, according to John."

I put down my clipboard. "That's awful. Did John say what happened?"

Cynthia shook her head. "No. Except the little girl was on her way to school." She paused. "One odd thing. It was another greyhound. A different one than Saturday's. This one was black, according to John."

Neither of us spoke for several seconds. Then I groaned.

"Oh dear," I said. "Dr. Augustin is going to be furious. He said when he volunteered to help out at the shelter, he meant spaying and neutering. Stuff like that. An occasional hit-by-car, maybe. Nothing controversial." I glanced over at the door to Dr. Augustin's office and lowered my voice. "Remember that cat-scratch-fever thing last year? Animal Control tried to get the mayor to institute a leash law for cats because of it. Dr. Augustin was called in as their 'expert.'"

Cynthia smiled very briefly. "I watched that commission meeting on TV. The chief of police asked the mayor if she thought arresting derelict cat owners was more important than arresting murderers, since he didn't have enough men to do both. As I recall, the paper wrote the whole thing up as a joke."

"They sure did," I said. "They made Dr. Augustin look pretty silly, because he supported the law." Life at the clinic had been almost unbearable for over a month.

Suddenly, Dr. Augustin called out. "*SaMANtha!* Would you please come in here?"

Cynthia and I looked at each other. Then I opened his door and went in.

Dr. Augustin was checking the contents of his medical bag. "Have Cynthia cancel my morning appointments," he said, without looking at me. "I should be back around one-thirty." He snapped the bag shut, then picked up his jacket and put it on. It was leather and smelled wonderful.

I wasn't sure if he was finished giving directions, so I continued to stand awkwardly in the middle of his office, mouth shut. All I could think about was whether or not he had overheard Cynthia and me talking about him.

He looked up. "Sam . . . those newspaper people"—with that tone of voice, he could have meant "those rapists" or "those tapeworms"—"may call or come by. You don't know anything and have no idea when I'll be back. Understand?"

He stared at me, his eyes boring a hole through my skull, the way they often did when he wanted to make a point. It was hard to tell where his pupils ended and his irises began, they were that dark. Women found his stare disarming, and he knew it and took full advantage of it when it suited him.

"I *don't* know anything," I said. "I don't even know who the girl was or whose dog it is."

"Okay," he said, turning his eyes off. "Thanks, Sam. I'll see you later. Hold down the fort." He grabbed his bag and left through the back door.

It took me a moment to get my thoughts together. I went out to the reception room and gave Cynthia the edict about talking to the press.

"You don't need to tell me," she said.

By lunchtime, we'd heard nothing from either the newspapers or Dr. Augustin. I was just settling down for my stint at the reception desk when an attractive, middle-aged man in gray slacks and a pink polo shirt came through the door. He carried a small notebook under his arm, and I became immediately suspicious. I put down my apple.

"May I help you?" I asked, guardedly.

He smiled. His eyes were pale blue, and there were tiny wrinkles at their corners, as if he smiled often. He had a nice tan and short, light brown hair, streaked with gray. He looked like he spent a lot of time outdoors. He certainly didn't *look* like a reporter. Of course, I didn't know what I was expecting, really.

"Good afternoon. My name is Michael Halsey. I'm with the *Times*." He held out his hand, and I shook it. It was warm and reassuring. Boy, was I a sucker, I thought, and tried to remember the edict.

"I'm Samantha Holt," I said. "I'm Dr. Augustin's technician."

"Technician?" he asked.

"Nurse," I replied.

"Oh, of course." He leaned against the reception desk, and I could smell his aftershave—fresh and woodsy. Nice. "Is Dr. Augustin around?" he asked.

"No," I answered. "He was called out unexpectedly, and I don't know when, or even if, he'll be back." I smiled. He smiled. This is a game, I thought, and I'm sure he's a lot better at it than I am.

"I understand that Dr. Augustin works part-time over at Animal Control."

"He helps out there on Wednesdays," I said. "Spaying and neutering, mostly."

He wrote something in his little notebook. "Is Dr. Augustin the veterinarian they contact whenever they have an emergency?"

Suddenly I remembered the time I was stopped by the police for doing fifty in a thirty-mile-an-hour zone. I hadn't talked my way out of that one, either.

"They usually contact the emergency clinic on Fifth Street," I responded, omitting the fact that the emergency clinic was only open at night and on weekends.

"I see," he said, still smiling. A few more notes in his little book. "Have you worked here long, Miss Holt?"

"About a year and a half," I said. My apple was turning brown.

"It must be very rewarding, taking care of people's pets." He closed his notebook and pushed his ballpoint into the book's little spiral binder. He reached out and offered me his hand. "Thank you for your time," he said. He sounded like he meant it. I shook the still-warm hand.

"You're most welcome," I told him. He turned and walked across the room. I noticed then that he wore canvas deck shoes and no socks. Not an Italian movie star, certainly, but appealing, nevertheless. He paused and looked back at me.

"Maybe I'll see you again sometime," he said. I looked at his left hand. No ring. Of course, that didn't necessarily mean anything. And why did I care if he was married?

"Maybe," I said, caring just a little.

He winked and went through the door. Suddenly I realized he hadn't told me why he was here and I hadn't asked, as if I'd already known. So, without saying it directly, I'd told him where Dr. Augustin was and why. Terrific. I picked up my apple.

Dr. Augustin hadn't shown up when our first appointment of the afternoon arrived—a stout, middle-aged, polyester-clad woman with faintly blue hair. The woman made no effort to hide her disappointment when Cynthia told her Dr. Augustin was out on an emergency. She brought her cat to the clinic once a month to have his nails trimmed. I usually did the trimming, but Dr. Augustin always managed to say a few words to the woman and pat the animal's head, as if it were a child.

This visit the woman's husband had come along. They could almost pass for twins, I thought with amusement, except his hair is shorter and less blue, and she is wearing a skirt. As I helped the woman with her cat I inclined my head in the man's direction and smiled. He grunted, then turned his attention to the magazine rack.

After the couple left, Cynthia called me over to her desk. "Dr. Augustin phoned a few minutes ago to say he wouldn't be in," she told me. "I'm supposed to call the rest of today's clients and reschedule them for tomorrow or Thursday. He's sending Larry Wilson to take the emergencies and walk-ins." She shook her head. "What if I can't reach everyone?"

I shrugged. "Let Larry take them. There's nothing especially complicated or serious lined up for this afternoon, is there?" I leaned over her shoulder and studied the appointment book, then chuckled. "Mad Max is coming in for his annual checkup. That should be interesting."

Mad Max was a two-hundred-pound mastiff with no obedience training. This made for a lovable, yet physically demanding patient. Drawing blood for a heartworm test was an exercise in survival training. Dr. Wilson would get quite a workout.

At that moment two cars pulled into the parking lot. Dr. Wilson stepped out of one of them and headed for the door. John Clark stumbled out of the other, aided by Mad Max, who then dragged his owner across the pavement, oblivious to the man's cries. Mr. Clark's arms looked as if they were being pulled from their sockets. Max's tongue was draped across his lower jaw, and foam covered his muzzle and chest like it would a Thoroughbred after a hard run.

Dr. Wilson had just gotten through the door, unaware of his pursuer, when I motioned for him to step aside. Max bounded through the partly open door, rattling the hinges and flinging his master against the door frame.

"Excuse me," Mr. Clark rasped. *"Max, sit!"* The dog raised his hind leg and marked the edge of Cynthia's desk with a stream of urine. Then he flopped on the floor, his back legs out behind him like a frog's, his tongue lolling. Dr. Wilson, looking like he had just seen the devil himself, vanished. Cynthia continued to update the Clark file, as if nothing unusual had happened.

After I cleaned up the "accident," I went in search of Dr. Wilson. He was in Dr. Augustin's office.

"What is that *horse* in here for?" he asked me as he fumbled with the lever of Dr. Augustin's toy bubblegum machine. "I thought this was a small-animal practice."

"It helps if you put a penny in it," I said.

"I don't have a penny, and why doesn't Lou fix it so you don't have to put money in it at all?"

I watched him as he searched for change on Dr. Augustin's desk. "Because we use the money to buy more gum. It's supposed to be self-supporting. Anyway, it'll take nickels, dimes, or quarters. Even Canadian money." I grinned.

He looked up at me, frowned, then took a quarter out of his pocket. "I should get twenty-five pieces of gum for this," he said, and shoved the coin into the machine. A small red ball dropped out. He put it in his mouth.

"Mad Max is here for his annual physical and vaccinations," I said, amused to see the color drain from Dr. Wilson's freckled face. "If you like, I could ask Mr. Clark to leave him for a couple of hours, and we could tranquilize him. He's really a very nice dog, just a bit exuberant."

I could tell Dr. Wilson felt this had merit. At twenty-six and less than a year out of vet school, Larry Wilson was not above admitting he couldn't do something. His experience with specimens like Mad Max was limited.

"Okay," he said. "Sounds like a good idea." He paused. "If Mr. Clark doesn't mind, of course."

I nodded and went out to the reception area.

Mr. Clark appeared overjoyed at my suggestion and made a hasty exit, as if I might suddenly change my mind.

"Why would the Clarks want a dog they couldn't control?" Cynthia asked, looking down at Max. He had fallen asleep, his great head flat on the floor between his front paws.

"I think he's supposed to be a watchdog. They keep him in the house, though, to keep him from getting fleas. I wonder what their furniture looks like."

"I wonder if they *have* furniture," Cynthia remarked. "I'll call Frank." She pressed the intercom, and I went back to Dr. Augustin's office.

"All set, Larry. Mr. Clark will be back at four-thirty."

Dr. Wilson was perusing one of Dr. Augustin's journals, his feet propped up on the desk. "Excellent, Sam. Thanks." He put the magazine down. "What other little surprises do you have in store for me?"

"How are you with parrots?" I asked.

Dr. Wilson sighed. "I knew I shouldn't have agreed to come in here today," he said, standing up. "My horoscope warned me to avoid confrontation." He spat his gum into the trash can. "Okay, let's get to it."

What a guy, I thought. I took Dr. Wilson's arm, and together we headed down the hall.

CHAPTER 3

•

The loose balcony railing outside my apartment chattered loudly against the stucco as I ran up the stairs.

Jeffrey Gamble, my neighbor and closest friend, opened his door and stuck out his beautiful, cherubic face, its halo of warm chestnut curls as unfettered as ever. "You're home early," he said. "And smiling, too. Augustin get flattened by a truck on his way to work today?"

I paused on the landing and frowned at him. "That's not funny, Jeff. And why aren't you out looking for a job?"

He followed me into my apartment, bending over to pick up my tiny, black-and-white cat, Tina, who along with her portly, dove-gray sister, Miss Priss, were waiting by the door like shoppers at a department-store grand-opening sale.

"I have been," he said. "You'll be happy to know I start Thursday." He put Tina down and opened my refrigerator. He pulled out a nearly full bottle of wine and got two glasses from the cabinet over the sink.

I went into my bedroom and closed the door. "Who on earth was foolish enough to hire you?" I yelled as I stripped off my uniform and climbed into a pair of jeans.

"Hey, I'll have you know I was this guy's first choice," he called back.

"His only choice, no doubt. You still haven't told me where." I pulled on a large sweatshirt that had a horse, a parrot, and a kitten painted on the front and LARGE OR SMALL, WE CARE FOR THEM ALL in big block letters. I opened the door.

"Freddy's Paradise Café," he said, handing me one of the wineglasses.

I took a sip, then grinned at him. "Well, at least you won't be over here raiding my refrigerator anymore."

Jeffrey flopped down on the sofa, his tall, wiry body sinking into the soft, overstuffed cushions. He was dressed in sweats and running shoes, his winter uniform. He was forever jogging through the neighborhood, even in the heat of summer. He'd gotten me into the habit, although five miles was my limit. I refused to enter any of the local races with him.

"I'm washing dishes," he said quietly, not looking at me. "For five bucks an hour."

I sat down beside him and put my hand on his arm. "Hey, there's nothing wrong with washing dishes. Or with five dollars an hour. I'm not making a whole lot more than that, myself, to 'scoop poop,' as they say. At least you have a chance to move up. Where am I going to go?"

"You could go to vet school," he offered, his glorious smile and sapphire eyes warming me as much as the wine.

"I don't think so. Not now, I'm too old." I turned to look at the reproduction hanging on the far wall. *Girl in Red with Her Cat and Dog*, by Ammi Phillips. Such a sweet face. She was strangling the poor cat, though. I finished my wine. "Besides, I'm through with school. Eighteen years is enough." I stood up, anxious to change the subject.

"So, how about an omelette for dinner?" I asked. "I assume you haven't eaten yet. Or did they feed you during the interview?"

He laughed. "How about me taking you out tonight? To celebrate my new career." He got up, flinging his arms out like wings, wine sloshing across my new ivory-and-green rug. I let it be. White wine wasn't so bad.

"You are looking at the future owner of Jeffrey's Steak House," he announced. "No . . . Jeffrey's Seaside Bar and Grill. That sounds more like me, don't you think?" He seemed pleased with himself. "So how about it?" he asked. "Dinner at the Rose and Crown? I promise I'll pay you back next week."

How could I refuse, even though I knew I'd never see the money again? I tried to remember how much cash I had. "All right," I said. "Let me get my purse."

I went quickly into the bedroom in search of my piggy bank.

Every bar stool at the Rose and Crown Pub was taken, and the crowd had spilled over into the dining room near the back of the building. We had to wait for a table. I amused myself watching the bartender. He was a handsome young man with several regular admirers—"groupies," according to Jeffrey—who always sat at the bar. One of them, a tiny brunette who looked anorexic she was so thin, sat perched like a sparrow next to the waitress stand. They smiled seductively at one another. It was disgusting.

After we were seated, Katherine came over to our table. "What'll it be, you two, food or drink?"

She was an attractive woman, around forty, although in the soft wash of the bar light, she could have been almost any age. She'd been in the States just since Christmas, but her English-porcelain complexion was already turning a deep honey color. You could see tiny white lines on her shoulders from the straps of her bathing suit.

"Both," Jeffrey announced enthusiastically. "A pitcher of McEwan's Export, definitely. And I'll have the fish and chips."

"The dinner salad for me," I said, "with ranch dressing. And maybe we should skip the pitcher, Jeffrey. Just have a couple of pints. I have to work tomorrow, don't forget."

"Nonsense," he said. "I'll drink whatever you don't want." He handed his menu to Katherine.

She winked and headed for the kitchen. Pretty soon she returned with a pitcher and two glasses. She poured mine, then Jeffrey's.

"Enjoy," she said. "Your food will be along presently." She went back to the bar.

I picked up my beer. This will be it, I told myself. Dr. Augustin is tough enough when I'm feeling good, let alone when I'm hung over.

Despite the crowd, our dinners came quickly, and Jeffrey dove right into the huge pile of oily "chips" on his plate that glistened like seasoned sunbathers. Before she left, Katherine topped off our glasses.

"Save room for trifle, Jeff," she said, grinning.

I stabbed a forkful of lettuce. "I wish I could eat like you do, Jeffrey," I said. "Where do you get the energy to run all the time?"

"That job of yours is wearing you out, Sam," he said. "You take Augustin way too seriously." He looked up from his plate. "What you need is a little romance in your life. You need a boyfriend."

I shook my head. "I *had* a boyfriend once, remember?"

"David was no boyfriend," Jeffrey said firmly. "David was simply an error in judgment, a mistake. We all make them." He leaned toward me, his expression somehow older, wiser. "You can't carry that around with you forever, Samantha. Not all men are creeps. Really."

I tried not to look at him. I knew if I did, I would smile, and I wanted to be angry. I wanted to scream and jump up and down and make hamburger out of every male in the room with blond hair who looked like David. I wanted them to know how I felt about being jilted for some airhead with fabulous tits and mile-long legs, whose biggest ambition in life was to marry someone with a Ferrari. A space cadet by the name of Lola, for God's sake.

I wanted them to know what it was like that perfect Saturday morning, standing in front of the mirror in the dressing room at St. Stephen's, my white Florentine satin gown sparkling in the light from the window. How I'd felt listening as the minister told my mother and me and six of my very closest friends that the groom wasn't coming. That he was sorry, but he'd changed his mind. That he wished me well, and I could keep the ring. The bastard couldn't even tell me himself. I'd taken the ring off and thrown all two and a half pear-shaped carats across the room. I told the minister he could keep it—use it to renovate the church's plumbing. Something really appropriate. He refused, of course. He said I'd feel differently after I cooled down. My mother agreed. She said she'd keep the ring in case I ever wanted to have the stone put into another setting. In case I wanted to melt down the gold. Fat chance. Maybe for dental fillings. Only in the soaps do people get left at the altar. It was a cliché, not real life.

Two hundred people waiting in the pews got to eat Cornish game hens with wild rice stuffing and drink champagne, anyway, and my mother had to pay for it. I couldn't bear to see my friends again, after that, despite the notes of consolation and endless stream of phone messages. Knowing that my father was up there in Hartford reading about it in the paper didn't make it any easier. So I left town—moved nearly two thousand miles away to avoid hearing the gossip, seeing the looks.

My father. He had dumped my mother for a twenty-six-year-old scrub nurse with bottled hair and breast implants, saying she made him feel young again. Male menopause, my mother had called it. Whatever the reason, I would never trust another man as long as I lived. But let's face it, I was bored. And lonely. I thought about Mrs. Winter. The idea that we might have something in common, after all, was strangely consoling.

I glanced up at Jeffrey and smiled. "I'm fine. Really." I drained my glass.

Jeffrey looked unconvinced, but he didn't say anything. He refilled my glass, then leaned back in his chair, hands clasped loosely across his middle. His face had taken on a sleepy, tranquil look.

"If you don't want to risk a real relationship," he said, "then how about a casual affair? It would do you a world of good, you know." He was serious.

I giggled. "Since I'm certain you're not offering yourself or any of your friends for this task, just exactly who did you have in mind?"

"I don't know, Samantha, but there's got to be *someone* you can date." He made it sound like I had some physical deformity or contagious disease.

I should have been offended, but I wasn't. Jeffrey meant well. I giggled again. There was something terribly amusing about his concern for my love life, but I couldn't quite pull it into focus. I took a drink of beer and got up. The room spun briefly.

"I have to go to the ladies'," I said. "I'll be right back."

I headed toward the rest rooms. Out of the corner of my eye, I saw Jeffrey signal Katherine. He was holding up our empty pitcher.

CHAPTER 4

•

Tuesday, February 8

I was aware of a whine coming from somewhere far away. I peered out from under my pillow. Miss Priss, her amber eyes barely three inches from my face, rose, stretched, and hopped off the bed. The whine continued—insistent, nagging. I looked down at the floor. My electric clock lay faceup like some trashed roadwise warning light. I hit the snooze bar, then closed my eyes. I had thirty minutes to get ready for work. Plenty of time.

Miss Priss jumped back onto the bed beside me. Her purring seemed unusually loud, and I retreated beneath my pillow. Then the alarm went off again. Reluctantly, I sat up. My brain began bobbing about in my head like a small boat on a rough sea. I made a mad, weaving dash for the bathroom.

Later, as I stood in the shower, cold water beating down on my head and neck, I vowed never to touch alcohol again. I wondered how Jeffrey was doing. There was no point in blaming him for my condition. I knew he'd just smile at me and say he was sorry—that he'd make it up to me and wasn't it good to get it all out of my system? If only I could remember exactly *what* I had gotten out of my system.

I arrived at the clinic fifteen minutes late. Cynthia looked at her watch, then at the Coke in my hand, and smiled.

"Tough night, huh?"

"Don't ask," I said. "Just tell me none of our surgeries showed up, and Dr. Augustin called in sick. Tell me we can all go home."

"No such luck," she answered. "Both spays are already here." She motioned toward Dr. Augustin's office. "One good thing—*he's* not in yet."

I headed for the lab, praying I would die right then and be spared the rest of the day.

At 9:15, Dr. Augustin marched through the front door, past the reception desk, and down the hall. Cynthia, P.J., and I stopped talking. He'd said "Good morning" without smiling, so we knew he really didn't mean it. P.J. scurried back into the lab like a roach escaping from an overturned log.

Cynthia grimaced and said quietly, "It's going to be a long day."

I figured things couldn't get much worse, so I went after him, mouth closed tight to avoid giving him an opening for sarcasm.

He was waiting in the surgery, our first patient on the table. The little beagle wagged her tail and lolled her tongue like she expected this to be a Sunday romp in the park. I clamped down on her and whispered in her ear while Dr. Augustin anesthetized her.

"Anything particularly earth-shattering happen yesterday?" Dr. Augustin asked, his back to me as he scrubbed. "Any reporters come snooping around?"

"A Michael Halsey from the *Times* was here, but left when he found out you weren't in."

"What did you tell him?" He slipped on his gown and

waited for me to tie it closed in back. His tone was accusatory.

"Nothing," I snapped. "You told me not to, so I didn't." I thought briefly about strangling him with the gown strings but remembered I still had twenty-four car payments to make.

Never one to apologize for anything, Dr. Augustin cleared his throat and deftly changed the subject. "Missy Meyerson looks a lot better this morning."

As he worked I cleaned off the countertop next to the refrigerator and listened to the quiet, even beating of the dog's heart, broadcast from the monitor on the wall behind me. I moved over to the sink, out of his field of vision.

"Was it from one of the kennels over at the track?" I asked. "The dog you had to euthanize."

I heard a loud metallic clank as Dr. Augustin threw one of his expensive German surgical instruments on the stainless-steel table. I held my breath.

"Yes," he said flatly. "It belonged to Rachel."

I wished I'd never brought it up. Rachel, Dr. Augustin's ex-wife, owned the Red Cavalier, a small farm north of Skelton. She raced greyhounds out of one of the kennels at the dog track. My impression was that she was a gutsy, determined woman, who would have been happier growing up if she'd been a boy, instead of just a tomboy.

Cynthia warned me never to mention Dr. Augustin's wife in his presence. She said the divorce was entirely Rachel's idea, and Dr. Augustin wanted her back, something she was having no part of, apparently.

I walked over to the table and turned down the flow of anesthetic gas. "Did the dog that attacked Missy Meyerson come from Rachel's kennel?"

"Yes," he said. "And now the people who adopted him

want Rachel to take him back." He finished closing the incision and began taking off his gloves. "The dog I put down yesterday, Black Magic, was one of her best dogs. What a waste."

"Do you think the little girl did something to provoke him?" I asked.

"Possibly. She's not in any position to say right now. Rachel told me someone left the kennel door open, and Magic slipped out. The kid lived in a trailer park about half a mile from the track."

He was washing his hands, his back to me. I began picking up the discarded instruments.

"Nobody saw the attack," he continued. "Animal Control went out and caught Magic later. He wasn't injured, but he had blood on him—the girl's blood, I guess."

The beagle started to wake up. I removed the tube from her throat and carried her to a recovery cage.

"How was Magic when you examined him?" I asked, trying to keep Dr. Augustin's attention focused on the matter at hand, rather than on me. I felt like I was moving in slow motion.

"He was nervous, dancing around in the cage, panting," Dr. Augustin said. "You'd expect that, though. He wasn't particularly hostile or aggressive. More like confused."

As if in a trance, I watched Dr. Augustin take a fresh spay pack out of the cabinet. I was still holding the beagle's endotrachial tube when he looked up. He stared at the tube, then at me.

"If it's okay with you, Samantha, I'd like to spay that little Siamese sometime before I retire." Then he looked more closely at my face and suddenly grinned. "If you're up to it, that is."

I pitched the tube in the sink and began spraying the table

with disinfectant. Smiling broadly, Dr. Augustin leaned against the wall and watched me. He's enjoying this, I thought angrily.

"So tell me, Sam, was there a crowd at the Rose and Crown last night?"

I groaned audibly and went out to get the Siamese.

The morning dragged on, relentlessly. At noon, Dr. Augustin went home for lunch, and I decided to take a nap on the daybed in his office. Cynthia volunteered to take my watch. I was grateful, since my hangover had reached the "walking dead" stage.

I was sound asleep when a loud noise in the reception room woke me. Suddenly Cynthia popped into Dr. Augustin's office, her face ashen. It took a lot to upset Cynthia, and I eyed her suspiciously.

"Sam," she shouted, "we need you out here!" I lifted myself up on one elbow.

"What's the matter?" I asked, not willing to deal with another Missy Meyerson.

"It's Rachel," she whispered, "with one of her dogs—Pogo—and it doesn't look good." When I didn't move immediately, her tone changed to one of exasperation. "Samantha, will you *please* get out here!"

There was, thankfully, no bloody cardboard carton. Instead, a great, fawn-colored greyhound lay sprawled on the floor, its noble head resting in Rachel Augustin's hand. Although the dog's eyes were open, its breathing was slow and shallow, and it showed no interest in getting up.

Rachel looked at me. She is a petite woman on the shy side of forty, who, at that moment, looked more like a little girl in her blue jeans and red "one size fits all" T-shirt. She has long, light brown hair and brown eyes that remind me of a spaniel's. Right then they sparkled with impending tears. She attempted a smile. At least she didn't look like she expected me to perform any veterinary miracles. Russell Curtis, her trainer, stood off to one side, wringing his hands bloodless.

"Let's get him into an exam room," I said, sliding my arms under the dog's rump

Russell bent over and gently lifted the animal's head and shoulders, and with Rachel close behind, we carried him into Room 1.

There was no way Pogo was going to fit on the exam table, sprawled out like he was, so we put him back on the floor. Rachel sat next to him and stroked his head. I reached for a thermometer.

"When I turned the dogs out at six-thirty this morning," Russell said, "I didn't think anything was wrong except he was tired." The man's voice was heavy with guilt. "He ran really super last night, losing the last race in a photo. It was only his second start at three eighths of a mile. We never expected him to do so well." He paused, looked down at Rachel, then back at me. "He had a little diarrhea on the way back to the kennel, at around eleven. Nothing serious. After he cooled down, I made sure he drank plenty of water. He was still pretty excited when I put him in his crate, barking and whining. And he wouldn't eat." Russell stuck his hands in his pockets. "I guess I should have brought him in first thing this morning."

Rachel was silent.

"His temperature is normal," I said. "Are any of the other dogs acting sick? Anybody else have diarrhea?"

"No . . . just Pogo." Russell slumped on the chair in the corner.

I drew a blood sample and was labeling the tube when Dr. Augustin arrived.

"Hello, Rachel," Dr. Augustin said softly. He turned to Russell and nodded, then took his stethoscope off its hook on the wall and knelt down beside Pogo. Without looking up, he said, "Sam, we need the results of that blood work ASAP."

As I turned to go I noticed that Rachel had moved over next to Dr. Augustin, her forearm just touching his knee.

We didn't discover anything significant from the lab tests. Dr. Augustin and I transferred Pogo to a bottom cage in Isolation and started him on intravenous fluids. By the time Russell left for the track, the dog had improved. Even so, Rachel said she wanted to hang around awhile longer, and Russell said okay, he would come back for her about four.

I caught only snatches of the conversation Rachel and Dr. Augustin were having in his office. Rachel was sitting in the armchair next to the desk, and Dr. Augustin had pulled his chair out in order to face her. They were quite close.

"This couldn't have happened at a worse time," Rachel said dismally. "It's taken me five years to get that adoption program established." Hugging her knees, she rocked back and forth in the chair. Dr. Augustin said nothing, but he opened and closed his fists like he did whenever he was nervous or frustrated.

"The public doesn't like euthanasia any more than I do," Rachel said. "It just seems like good business sense to put greyhounds up for adoption instead of killing them, when they can't run." She put her feet back on the floor. "I had a hard time convincing the other owners, though, because of all the damned paperwork, but they finally agreed to participate." Her voice wavered. "Now people will be afraid to bring the dogs into their homes. And that's ridiculous. Magic *couldn't* have hurt that little girl. There's got to be a mistake."

Rachel started to cry, and Dr. Augustin quickly took her hand and was consoling her when Cynthia called me to the reception desk.

The waiting room was full, and I kept busy taking histories and weighing animals. Dr. Augustin stayed with Rachel, leaving her only long enough to give an injection or write a prescription. I was beginning to get annoyed. My hangover was still with me, and the fact that I hadn't eaten anything substantial in over thirty-six hours didn't help my mood one bit.

At four, Russell arrived. After saying good-bye and telling Rachel to call him when she got home, Dr. Augustin disappeared into Room 2. Rachel took one last look at Pogo, and she and Russell left. I went out to the reception area to get our next patient.

I was standing to one side with my arms folded, waiting for the client to gather up her things, when I saw an unmarked police car, with its conspicuous black sidewall tires and telltale yellow CITY license tag, pull up. A tall, youngish-looking man with brown hair pulled back in a short ponytail got out. He was dressed a lot like Dr. Augustin, in jeans and a T-shirt. He had a gold police badge hanging from his left jeans pocket and a holstered pistol clipped securely onto his belt.

"Detective Stephen Weller to see Dr. Augustin," I heard him say to Cynthia.

A hush fell over the waiting room as six bored and impatient people, holding an assortment of equally impatient pets, waited to see what the police wanted with their veterinarian. Cynthia glanced at me, and I motioned for her to stay put, that I would tell Dr. Augustin.

"There's a man out front to see you," I whispered, when he opened the exam-room door. "Say's he's a cop, though he sure doesn't look like one." I waited for him to growl at me, but he just sucked a bunch of air through his teeth and looked disgusted.

"Ask him to wait in my office," he told me. "I'll get to him when I get to him." He shut the door.

I went back out to the reception room and showed the detective into Dr. Augustin's office. "Can I get you a cup of coffee?" I asked him. His hair looked clean, at least, and his fingernails were neatly trimmed. He'd look a lot better if he smiled, I thought.

He shook his head. "No, thank you." He glanced nervously around the room and then at his watch. "Will Dr. Augustin be long?" he asked. He looked like he had a train to catch.

"I don't think so," I answered. "Please"—I motioned toward the chair next to Dr. Augustin's desk—"have a seat." He remained standing. I shrugged and walked out through the lab.

A few minutes later I heard Dr. Augustin telling the client in Room 2 good-bye, and I quickly finished what I was doing.

He and the detective were talking when I got to the doorway connecting his office with the lab. P.J. was bent over her microscope, but I could tell she was eavesdropping. She looked up, and I put a finger to my lips.

Dr. Augustin was sitting at his desk, turned so he could see the detective, who was still standing.

"And how did the dog act when you first examined him?" Weller asked.

Dr. Augustin's face was impossible to read. "Nervous, frightened, jumpy." He stood up. "Greyhounds are not vicious dogs, Detective. They sometimes chase small animals like cats, because that's their nature, but they are not trained to attack and kill like some breeds." He walked over to the reception-room door and opened it, seeming to imply that the interview was finished. "I don't know what possessed Magic to attack that little girl. Maybe she threw a rock at him. Maybe there was another dog involved." He waited for the detective to leave.

"Well . . . thank you . . . Doctor." He suddenly tore a piece of paper from a little notebook and jotted something down on it. He handed it to Dr. Augustin. "If you can think of anything else, anything that might help us understand what happened, please call me. I can be reached day or night at one of those numbers." He paused, then went out, and Dr. Augustin shut the door.

P.J. was still staring into the microscope at her now dried-up slide and did not look up as Dr. Augustin trudged across the hall into Room 1.

At this rate, I thought, we are going to be here all night.

CHAPTER 5

•

Thursday, February 10

The clinic is closed Wednesdays. One of Cynthia's nephews goes in to clean and feed. Dr. Augustin does treatments, which is fortunate, since I spent most of that Wednesday in bed.

Thursday was chaotic, to say the least. Dr. Augustin complained all morning, mostly about Cynthia double-booking appointments, conveniently forgetting that it was his fault in the first place. She finally lost her temper and told him the next time he decided to go AWOL, he could reschedule his own clients. After that, he kept quiet. The damage was done, however, and we all walked around the rest of the day like a big, ugly cloud had spoiled our picnic.

Just before lunch, while we were x-raying a German shepherd puppy, I got up the nerve to ask him about Pogo.

"I'll never be able to prove anything," Dr. Augustin said. "Not without the proper tests. And now it's too late, of course."

We stood behind the lead shield and I took the radiograph.

"Tests?" I asked.

Dr. Augustin went over to the table and pulled out the film cassette. He handed it to me, and I stepped into the darkroom.

"I think Pogo was given some type of stimulant an hour or so before he was scheduled to race," he said through the door.

I came out of the darkroom. We stood by the X-ray table while the automatic processor gurgled and squeaked contentedly.

Dr. Augustin continued. "From what Russell said—the nervousness and diarrhea, the loss of appetite. Then crashing like he did after it wore off. It sure points to a stimulant overdose. Amphetamines, probably."

I handed him the radiograph, and he put it up on the view screen.

"Who would do that?" I asked. "It's illegal."

I couldn't imagine Rachel involved in anything crooked, especially if it meant drugging one of her dogs. It always seemed to me that she put the welfare of her animals above everything else. In any case, I wasn't going to suggest her as a potential suspect.

"Of course it's illegal," he said. "But banned substances are a part of every sport. Although it isn't nearly as common in greyhound racing as in horse racing, it's bound to occur." As if reading my mind, he added, "Rachel would never do it. The question is, who else would want to improve Pogo's chances?"

The ghostly image on the screen played across Dr. Augustin's face, accentuating the sharp contours of his nose and chin. In the pale fluorescent glow, he looked almost predatory.

"Are you going to tell her?" I asked.

He shrugged. "She may already have reached the same conclusion herself." He turned back to the dog on the table. "Let's get another view, before he wakes up."

• • •

We didn't discuss the matter again that day. The next afternoon, Rachel came in with Joker, another one of her dogs.

"He was going too fast at the first turn and overshot it and slid into the fence," Rachel explained. "Nothing seems to be broken, but when I took off his muzzle, he bit me and one of the leadouts." She stood in the exam room, her right hand wrapped in a fresh white bandage. "As you can see, he's bouncing off the walls."

Joker was a red brindle male, with an interesting dark patch over one eye that made him look like a pirate. His race name was Red Jokers Wild. I had seen him once before, when he'd come into the clinic to have a torn ear repaired. I remembered him as a calm, gentle dog, who stood quietly while we worked on him. Right then he was anything but calm.

Rachel had wisely put the dog's muzzle back on, but Dr. Augustin took it off. It made panting difficult, and Joker was panting so hard he had started to wheeze. He danced from one foot to the other and strenuously resisted when Dr. Augustin tried to clamp his mouth closed in order to listen to his chest.

"Take him outside, Sam," he said to me, "and see if he'll give us a urine sample." He put the dog's muzzle back on.

We went out the back way. Joker's wheezing was so pronounced, I was afraid someone passing by would hear it and wonder what frightful things we did to our patients.

After prancing about, wild-eyed, Joker lifted his leg against a telephone pole, and I whipped my cup under him. He never noticed.

Back in the exam room, I saw that Dr. Augustin had

gotten out a bottle of Valium and had drawn some up in a syringe. Rachel was sitting on the floor in the corner.

"We'd better refrigerate that sample," Dr. Augustin said, "until I can figure out where to send it." He gave Joker the injection and took the dog's muzzle off. I labeled the container and took it into the lab. When I got back, Rachel was talking.

"I'm almost positive it was Brad Donovan's voice," she said. I stood by the door, and all three of us watched her dog like we expected him to disappear or turn a strange color or something.

"He told me I would regret talking to the others. That I should keep my mouth shut and mind my own business. I told Tom Rheems, the track's new assistant manager, about the meat. He was sympathetic and said he would look into it, but he cautioned me to keep a low profile—that it might stir up the public if the newspapers got wind of it. He said the industry couldn't stand another animal-cruelty incident, no matter how contrived. He was right, of course."

Joker had stopped panting and now was lying on the floor.

"Meat?" I asked tentatively. I felt like I often had as a child around my father's friends—out of place, in the way. Rachel looked up, seeming to notice me for the first time, and smiled faintly.

"I was telling Lou that most of us at the track buy the beef we feed our dogs from Bayside Meats, here in town. In truth, we don't have much choice. The only other local place that sells bulk meat for animals is across the bay, and they charge five cents more per pound. I usually get about six hundred pounds a week, so it's a big difference."

Joker sighed, stretched, and closed his eyes.

Rachel got up. "About a month ago, I noticed that the

quality of what Bayside was sending me had gone way down. I complained, and they said if I didn't like it, I could take my business elsewhere. Well, I can't afford to go anyplace else, and they know it." She started pacing back and forth.

"I talked to a few of the other owners, and they all agreed the meat looked pretty bad. But they can't afford to switch companies, either. Anyway, that's when I got the phone calls telling me to keep quiet."

Dr. Augustin reached out and put his hand on her shoulder, but she shrugged it off.

"Well, I won't keep quiet." She spun around, her eyes uncharacteristically cold. "That stuff from Bayside is mostly skin and fat. It smells half-spoiled and has freezer burn all over it. None of the dogs has gotten sick yet, but it can't be very nutritious. I've increased the supplements I normally mix with it, but supplements are expensive, too." She sat down again, this time on the chair. "Maybe a boycott is in order. With the exception of Donovan, I can probably persuade the other owners and trainers to pay the higher price Ascott Foods charges for a month or so. That should get Bayside's attention."

"How does the stuff make it through inspection?" I asked.

Dr. Augustin was leaning against the wall, watching Rachel. "It doesn't have to," he said. "Not if it's been decharacterized." I stared at him. "Mixed with powdered charcoal and labeled 'Not for Human Consumption.'" He picked up his stethoscope and knelt down beside Joker. "All a slaughterhouse has to do is decharacterize it and ship it directly to a pet-food processor. That way it bypasses the normal inspection process."

He listened to Joker's heart, then stood up. "It's usually cattle that have died on the feedlot, but it might be horse meat or kangaroo, and few people would know. Or care, for that matter. Most of the time the stuff is okay."

I heard the phone ring and went to the reception room to see if our three o'clock appointment had shown up. Through the glass, I saw Detective Weller pull into the parking lot.

"That cop is back," I told Cynthia, thankful there were no clients waiting.

She turned her head and watched him get out of his car. "He's kind of cute, don't you think?" she asked. "Like one of those undercover policemen you see in the movies. I wonder if he's married."

I smiled. "I'll go tell Dr. Augustin he has company," I said, pointedly ignoring her. "This should make his day."

Detective Weller wanted to know about the biting incident at the track and what was being done with the dog. Dr. Augustin handled himself pretty well, I thought, considering he had to leave out most of what he knew and all of what he suspected.

After the detective drove off and our 4:15 appointment came and went, I asked Dr. Augustin why he thought a detective would bother following up on a dog bite.

"Why don't they just send a patrolman?" I asked. I was in the lab filling prescriptions. Rachel was back at the track. She'd left Joker at the clinic for observation. Dr. Augustin didn't like the way the dog's heart sounded, although he said he doubted the problem was permanent.

"Who knows? Maybe they see a connection between Magic and this thing with Joker." Dr. Augustin stared into P.J.'s microscope at one of her blood smears. P.J. was in the kennel, "helping Frank," apparently finding our would-be rock star's company preferable to being told her technique needed polishing.

"Is there a connection?" I asked. "Did someone drug Magic, too? Is that why he attacked that little girl?"

Dr. Augustin looked up from the microscope. "Too much time had elapsed for Magic's anxiety to be a result of a stimulant overdose," he answered. "Assuming he was given the drug before his race Saturday night, that is." He spun around on his stool. "I wonder how he did Saturday."

He slid off the stool and went into his office. I could hear him talking. In a few minutes he reappeared in the doorway.

"Magic came in sixth," he said. "He was dead on his feet, according to Russell." He stood there a minute, staring over my head at nothing in particular. "How interesting," he said finally.

"What is?" I asked.

"A tranquilizer, like chlorpromazine—Thorazine—might cause a dog to act aggressive or vicious," he explained. "Even forty-eight hours after the drug is administered. It's unusual, but certainly not unheard of."

I thought about this for a minute. "You mean, someone really *is* trying to fix those races?" I asked, amazed that anyone would bother. After all, greyhound racing was hardly in the same league as the Kentucky Derby.

"Possibly," he answered. "Or trying to make it look like Rachel is."

So it was back to the dog food, again, was it? I started to say there must be big money in ground kangaroo, but Cynthia stuck her head around the corner to announce our last client of the day, and I let it go.

CHAPTER 6

•

Friday, February 11

I hate Fridays. Even though I get paid then, and even if I didn't have to work the next day, I would still hate Fridays, dread them, in fact. Actually, I only dread the second and fourth Fridays of the month. The Brightwater Beach City Commission meets the second and fourth Thursday. Since Dr. Augustin is never happy with what transpires at those meetings, he always comes to work the next morning with an attitude. "Biweekly PCMS," I call it—"post-commission-meeting syndrome." Unfortunately, time is the only cure.

"Have you seen this morning's City and State section?" Cynthia asked me after she had put away her purse and coat. Dr. Augustin was late.

"No," I said, "but let me guess. The commission voted down the police substation."

"Sure did. Three to two."

"Terrific," I said glumly. We went into the lab for coffee. "Did the paper give it much coverage? Or did they bury it on page seven?"

"No. Amazingly, it was the lead story," Cynthia said. "It seems there was quite a long discussion with a huge contingent from the project there in favor of the substation. Mothers, mostly, complaining about the number of shootings that occur. Of course no one with any political clout was there to support them. Money was the reason it didn't pass. Either Dr. Augustin didn't say anything, or the paper left out his statement. Probably the latter, since I can't imagine him not putting in his two cents' worth, can you?"

Dr. Augustin shouted Cynthia's name, and she turned to go. I put my coffee cup in the sink. "If you need me, I'll be in the bathroom," I said, and fled.

When I came out, I heard him clanking around in the surgery. Figuring I had better get in there before he totally ransacked the place, I took a deep breath and went across the hall.

He looked up when I came in. "Samantha, where the hell is my eye pack? And it had better be sterile." He slammed yet another drawer, rattling its contents.

I stepped calmly over to the surgery table and pointed at the tray. The pack in question was sitting there, waiting for him. I resisted the temptation to be smart.

"So," he said, obviously embarrassed, "where is our patient? Time is money, you know."

I carried the cocker spaniel to a recovery cage and closed the door. Dr. Augustin hadn't said three words to me during the entire procedure. In spite of his black mood, he had quickly and skillfully repaired the dog's eyelid, apparently with little or no effort. He continued to amaze me. It was like he had a little switch in his head, and he could turn off whatever was bothering him. But only long enough to finish the job at hand.

"And I thought that woman had more sense," he said suddenly. The switch obviously was back in the "On" position.

Since I didn't have the faintest idea who he was talking about, I kept quiet.

"Siding with an asshole like Stanley Tohlman is not going to get my vote come time for reelection, I can tell you that!" He yanked on a paper towel, causing the entire roll to fall into the sink. "I don't care how convincing his argument was about fiscal responsibility," he continued. "Sloan Avenue needs that police substation. The drug dealers are taking the place over."

"Maybe the mayor doesn't care," I said. "Maybe public housing projects can't compete with upscale communities like Pine Bluffs. Maybe she figures no one will complain if a few welfare recipients bump each other off."

"I find that hard to believe," he said, retrieving the roll of paper towels and snapping it back in place. "She always impressed me as being above that sort of thing. Unfortunately, Commissioner Tohlman failed to mention the fact that Sloan Avenue is the most direct route to that new soccer complex up by the high school. And some white kid's mom is going to get shot one day passing through the project on her way to practice." He peered at the cocker spaniel through the cage bars.

"Tohlman would rather have every resident carry a gun and a fire extinguisher," he said, "than spend another nickel expanding the police and fire departments. It might mean we wouldn't have the funds to support major-league baseball. God forbid."

If ever there was a good time to ask Dr. Augustin about his intention to run for a seat on the City Commission, this was it. But before I could open my mouth, Frank stuck his head around the corner to say he had a dog in the tub who was seizuring. Dr. Augustin raced out, telling me to bring along the Valium and a syringe, and my chance was gone.

CHAPTER 7

•

Saturday, February 12

Michael Halsey dropped by at noon. "Hello, again, Miss Holt," he said as he came in the door. He was wearing a pale blue, long-sleeve cotton shirt, with a button-down collar, navy slacks, and penny loafers.

We shook hands, and I noticed that his was as warm as ever. I was glad I had combed my hair before taking my turn at the front desk.

"Hello," I said, smiling. I pushed aside my container of cottage cheese. "What can I do for you?"

Dr. Augustin was in his office eating a cheeseburger and fries. He hadn't cautioned us about talking to the enemy, but I knew better than to bring up the drug thing. That didn't leave much for the press to misquote. It didn't leave much for them to be interested in really, when you got right down to it, and I wondered why Halsey was there.

"I happened to be in the area and thought I would stop by and inquire about the dog that bit those two people at the track yesterday." He wasn't carrying his little notebook. "I understand you've got him here in the hospital."

The telephone interrupted us. Halsey occupied himself reading the little brochures lying around the room. He peered at the dog heart preserved in a mayonnaise jar that sat on Cynthia's desk like a trophy, his nice tan turning slightly greenish. Dozens of long, thin, white worms stuck out of the heart's pulmonary artery like so many snakes on Medusa's head. It was intended to shock dog owners into getting their pets tested for heartworms. It usually succeeded, which was why Dr. Augustin put it in the reception area, even though Cynthia said it made her sick.

"What *is* that thing—a heart?" Halsey asked, after I'd hung up the phone.

I nodded. "A golden retriever's," I told him. I grimaced sympathetically. "Pretty disgusting, isn't it?"

Halsey moved away from the jar and cleared his throat. "Where were we?" he asked, smiling. "Oh yes, the greyhound you have in the hospital." He leaned casually against the reception desk. "Was he hurt, or just ticked off about losing?" The crinkles at the corners of his eyes and his smile gave him away.

"You're not really interested in that dog, are you?" I asked, laughing.

"Not really," he said. "I just dropped by for a little professional advice."

"What kind of advice?"

"I'd like to purchase a pet for my niece, and I thought perhaps you could suggest something."

I leaned back in my chair and studied his face. I had to admit, his come-on was original.

"How old is your niece?" I asked, playing along.

"She'll be six in May." He took out his wallet and flipped through the credit cards, driver's license, and other assorted necessities of everyday life, until he found what he'd been looking for. He held the photograph out so I could see it. A cute little girl with sandy blond hair and expressive gray eyes smiled back at me. There was a strong family resemblance.

"Cute kid," I said. "Does she live in a house with a yard or in an apartment?"

"A condo," he said. "And I think a dog is out of the question, unless it's a little dog. My sister and her husband both work. Kelly stays with a sitter."

We talked about several possibilities and decided on a kitten. He said he would speak to his sister and thanked me for my time. As he was leaving he asked me if I would be at work Monday, that he might give me a call to discuss the matter further. I said, "Sure, unless I win the lottery." He smiled and left, and I found myself looking forward to his call, even if it was about his niece.

CHAPTER 8

•

Monday, February 14

It was Valentine's Day. Cynthia had made cookies in the shape of little hearts, and she brought two dozen of the evil, buttery-rich, thickly iced things in for me to look at and smell all morning, before finally succumbing. Cynthia, like my mother, is a wicked person, deep down.

Dr. Augustin, who normally indulges in anything that is bad for him, especially if Cynthia makes it, stayed clear of the cookies. It was almost as if by eating one, he would have to acknowledge the existence of Valentine's Day.

He was also, predictably, none too pleased by the results of Joker's urinalysis. He'd sent the sample via Federal Express to a lab up in Gainesville, where a college buddy of his worked. Dextroamphetamine, the report stated.

Midmorning, a delivery boy from The Petal Pushers brought a small pink-and-white flower arrangement, addressed to me. The card read, *Thanks for being my friend. Jeff.* I handed the card to Cynthia.

"It's nice Jeffrey finally got a job," I said. "Now I won't have to pay for these."

Cynthia shook her finger at me and clucked her tongue. "When will you learn it's the thought that counts?"

"Yes, Mother," I said and went into the lab.

Around eleven, with the waiting room full of clients and

Dr. Augustin half an hour behind schedule, a tall woman in her early fifties wearing a slim-cut Liz Claiborne skirt and jacket set came in the door. She was leading a typically nervous, toe-tapping standard poodle. Black as tar.

I had never seen her before, and she didn't have an appointment. I couldn't hear what Cynthia said to her, but I knew we didn't have time to see her dog, unless it was an emergency. The woman looked upset.

Cynthia came around from behind the desk and motioned for me to follow her down the hall. We stopped in front of the lab.

"Unless we want to work straight through lunch, I don't see how I can squeeze this Rheems woman in until four-thirty at the earliest. She says her dog, Pepe, has an ear infection and is in severe pain. She feels that constitutes an emergency." Cynthia frowned. "What should I do?"

"I take it she hasn't been here before," I said, suddenly aware of something tickling my memory. "What did you say her name was?"

"Rheems, Mrs. Thomas," she answered. "From somewhere over in Pine Bluffs. She didn't give me her first name. Like *Mrs.* Thomas Rheems was supposed to carry more weight."

It might be a coincidence, I thought, but two Thomas Rheemses living in the exclusive Pine Bluffs subdivision next to the dog track was unlikely.

"You'd better stick her in somewhere this morning." I looked at my watch. "What there is left of it. Trust me. Dr. Augustin will want to see her." I dashed off, avoiding the daggers I knew Cynthia's eyes were discharging in my direction.

Mrs. Rheems, I thought. Now why on earth would she

bring her dog to Dr. Augustin instead of to a vet nearer the track?

I told Dr. Augustin about the change in schedule. "I thought you'd probably want to see her," I said.

He rolled his eyes and sighed heavily. "I suppose. Maybe if we cater to Mrs. Rheems, Rachel will be able to get some action out of Mr. Rheems on that Bayside problem of hers."

Dr. Augustin gave Pepe a thorough physical, spending considerably more time with Mrs. Rheems than was normal for a new-client appointment. He fawned over her dog and turned on his eyes full throttle. Mrs. Rheems was completely enchanted, which was the plan, no doubt. She said she had been looking for a veterinarian for her darling Pepe and had heard that Dr. Augustin was one of the best. She didn't say who had told her, and Dr. Augustin didn't ask.

Mrs. Rheems—Sylvia to Dr. Augustin—reminded me of Mrs. Winter. They both had expensive tastes, but Sylvia lacked Glynnis's style. My mother would say that Glynnis was old money, and Sylvia was more the "nouveau riche" type. Glynnis Winter's arrogance was polished to perfection. There was a degree of uncertainty in Mrs. Rheems's haughtiness.

"You be sure to call me right away if Pepe's ear doesn't improve in a day or two, Mrs. Rheems . . . Sylvia," Dr. Augustin said as he washed his hands, his back to her.

She smoothed down an invisible wrinkle in her skirt and fluffed her hair. "I certainly will, Doctor, don't you worry."

I handed her Pepe's leash, and she snapped it onto the dog's collar without looking at me. I'll bet she has trouble keeping servants, I mused, and smiled at the spot of grease on the back of her shell-pink skirt.

Dr. Augustin made a few more notes in Pepe's file, then escorted Mrs. Rheems out to the reception desk, where she took a bit too long, I thought, to shake his hand. She paid Cynthia in cash and, with her dog beside her on the front seat, drove off in her white Mercedes.

For the next two hours we barely had time to breathe. Just as Cynthia had predicted, lunchtime came and went with only Frank able to get away. At two o'clock, the young man from the florist shop reappeared, this time carrying a huge cut-glass vase containing a dozen white roses. The card read *To my favorite veterinary nurse. Mike.*

I tried to stay calm and act like this sort of thing happened to me every day. Unfortunately, I grinned all the way through our next two patients, even though one of them was an obnoxious African gray parrot who tried to bite my finger off and succeeded in nailing Dr. Augustin instead. Dr. Augustin promptly lost his temper and instructed me to get my flowers out of the lab. That the place was starting to look like a mortuary. I was tickled pink.

Things finally slowed down by about four. Rachel came in to visit with Joker and to find out about the urinalysis. She was dressed in a denim jumpsuit and work boots. Her hair was pulled back in a ponytail.

"How could somebody slip drugs to your dog without being seen?" I asked her.

"It wouldn't be too difficult," she said as she scratched Joker's head. She was sitting cross-legged on the floor in Isolation, and Joker was trying unsuccessfully to curl up in her lap. "Someone could shove a pill or capsule into a little chunk of meat and give it to a dog in the ginny or on the way to the starting box. No one would be the wiser."

"Ginny?" I asked.

"It's a sort of holding area where all the dogs scheduled to run are kept until race time. Some of them could be in there for up to five hours or more. Only one or two track officials are allowed in the ginny. It's supposed to guarantee the dogs aren't messed with. But, you never know." She stood up as Dr. Augustin came in the room.

"How do they know if a dog's been 'messed with'?" I asked. "Or do they?"

"The luck of the draw, I guess. A state guy takes urine samples from a couple of the dogs at the end of each race. The winner and one other. Sometimes it's the loser, sometimes not. My dogs haven't been checked lately." She stared down at Joker. "But somebody sure wants me to get caught. I guess if they keep drugging my dogs, it'll happen sooner or later." Dr. Augustin put his hand on her arm, and she didn't seem to mind this time.

"What would happen," I asked, "if they found a banned substance?"

"Russell would catch the flack, because as trainer, he's responsible for the dogs at race time. He'd get fined, and the track probably wouldn't renew my lease." She led Joker back to his cage. "I've got to go."

"We're done for the afternoon, aren't we, Sam?" Dr. Augustin looked over at me and smiled.

"Sure," I said, hoping he noticed the sarcasm in my voice. "I'll do treatments and lock up."

"Thata girl," he told me over his shoulder as he and Rachel headed for his office. He hadn't noticed. "See you in the morning."

"Yeah," I said.

Before P.J. and I left, at five minutes to five, the phone rang. I grabbed the hall extension. Cynthia was trying to figure out why she had thirty dollars more than the computer said she was supposed to have, and didn't look like she needed the aggravation of a phone call.

"Paradise Cay Animal Hospital," I said.

Michael Halsey's voice struck me from the other end like a fist. "Samantha, is that you?" He sounded out of breath. "Listen, I'm sorry to be calling right at quitting time, but they sent me out to do a story on a boating accident over by Sunset Beach, and I just this minute walked in the door."

"Oh, that's okay," I said dumbly. I tried to think. "The roses—they're beautiful."

"I'm glad you like them."

"Did you talk to your sister?" I asked, eager to direct the conversation toward something less threatening.

"About what? Oh—the kitten. No, not yet. I just haven't had the time."

An uncomfortable silence ensued, like the lull between breakers on a beach. Then I heard him inhale sharply.

"The reason I called, Samantha, was to see if you had any plans for Friday night?"

Why was I surprised at this, when his asking me out was all I'd thought about for the last three days? Why was I now looking for some way to tell him, yes, I had plans already? Wouldn't that be safer? It would certainly be easier. Then I looked into Isolation at Joker dozing in his cage, his long legs curled up under him like a cat's. The cage tag read, simply, AUGUSTIN.

"Friday? No, I don't think so," I said.

"Would you like to go out to dinner?"

"That would be nice," I said.

"Super. I'll give you a call later in the week, and we'll decide on a time and place. Right now I have to go. Duty calls." He laughed.

"Bye . . . Michael," I responded, testing the sound and feel of his name on my tongue. "Thank you, again, for the roses."

"You're welcome, again. Good-bye, Samantha." He was gone.

I stood in the hall, holding the receiver in my hand, for what seemed like a full minute, before P.J. finally took it from me and hung it back up.

"Are you all right, Sam?" she asked, peering into my face.

I looked down at her and smiled. "Oh, I'm fine," I said calmly. "I have a date this Friday."

P.J. clapped her hands, then grabbed me and gave me a hug. "Wow, that's absolutely fantastic, Samantha!" she exclaimed.

I glared at her. She acted like it was some kind of miracle or something. God, I thought, I can hardly wait to tell Jeffrey.

CHAPTER 9

•

Friday, February 18

I had a dental appointment that morning and didn't get to the clinic until 11:15. All four of our ten-to-eleven clients were sitting in the reception room, their patience obviously worn thin. I glanced questioningly at Cynthia, who was on the phone. Her expression made me think twice about going any farther. But, after mumbling vague apologies all around, I headed for the lab.

P.J. was standing at the sink washing test tubes. She looked terrible. Her face was puffy, and the glow from her nose could have lit Tampa Stadium.

"Are you okay?" I asked.

She shook her head. "No," she said, "I'm not. It's this cold. I should have stayed home, but I knew you'd be at the dentist." She grabbed a tissue and blew. "Anyway, now that I'm here, I might as well tough it out." She grinned feebly and held up a telltale brown paper bag. "At least I can't smell anything."

"They're backing up out front," I said. "Where is Dr. Augustin?"

P.J. cringed. "He's in the surgery doing a necropsy."

I felt my stomach contract. "Oh, on whom?"

"One of Rachel's dogs. She brought it in a couple of hours ago. It was already dead."

I dropped the coffee cup I'd just taken off the shelf. It shattered, and pieces skittered across the floor in all directions. I began gathering up the fragments nearest the door, when Cynthia appeared, looking like she expected to see something corrosive eating its way through the linoleum.

"What happened?" she asked.

"Nothing," I said. "I dropped my coffee cup." I stood up, hands full of pottery shards, and motioned toward the surgery. "Was it Joker?"

Cynthia shook her head. "No, it's Red Cavalier. Rachel said he was fine last night, although he didn't run very well." She lowered her voice and glanced over her shoulder into the hall. "Dr. Augustin thinks somebody killed him."

I sighed and dumped the remains of my cup in the trash. Red Cavalier III, better known as R.C., was Rachel's biggest winner. He was also her favorite.

"I guess I'll go see if he needs any help," I said.

Dr. Augustin was staring into the greyhound's abdominal cavity. He glanced up at me as I stepped cautiously into the room.

"Sam, come look at this," he said. He didn't sound the least bit angry or upset. Actually, he sounded pretty excited—like he was enjoying himself—and I found this somewhat disconcerting.

I went over to the table. The dog's intestines had been neatly laid out on a drape, and Dr. Augustin had made a longitudinal incision down their entire length.

"What do you see?" he asked.

Holding my breath, I peered at the inner lining of the small intestine. Tiny colored spheres dotted the tissues like beads on a gown. "Are those from some kind of time-release capsule?" I asked, after I'd stepped away from the carcass.

"You bet," he said. "Probably Thorazine. I'll send a sample up to Bob, but that's what I think it is. They must have given him several doses after the first capsule didn't do the trick. A tablet would have been more efficient. Or an injection. He died sometime during the night. My guess is they never intended to kill him, but got impatient." He took a specimen jar from the shelf behind him, carefully scraped a few of the beads into it, then handed it to me. "Same label as before," he said.

"Surely Rachel will get some action out of Rheems now," I said, taking the jar.

"I don't know if she's even mentioned the problem to him. She's convinced the state will blame her for the drugs." He had put the greyhound back together, more or less, and was washing his hands. "Let's face it, the odds have been shaken up by her most recent entries. Actually, I'm surprised she hasn't gotten caught yet." He dried his hands, then took a black plastic bag out of the cabinet. With some effort, he began pulling it around the dog's body.

I went over to help him. "Maybe she should confront that Donovan guy, or whoever she thinks is responsible. Tell him to lay off or she'll go to the cops, or something."

"I think she may do just that. She left here this morning madder than I've ever seen her. I told her to be careful, but then Rachel never *did* listen to me." He shook his head. "She's one stubborn lady."

I tried not to smile, but had to turn away. Look who's calling the kettle black, I thought. "Why don't you go to Rheems?" I asked.

Dr. Augustin shot me a glance that would have wilted a cactus. "Do I look crazy?" He closed the bag with a tie. "No way. If Rachel wants my help, she'll ask for it. Otherwise, it's her call."

He hefted the bag off the table and headed for the kennel, where we kept a large, chest freezer. I was glad the guys from the crematory came by on Fridays.

Dr. Augustin paused in the doorway. "Put our first patient in a room and tell the client I'll be right there," he said.

I couldn't believe it. I'd finally found someone Dr. Augustin was afraid of. All ninety-five pounds of her.

Michael Halsey didn't call until two. I'd almost given up on him. I was cleaning the exam rooms in preparation for the afternoon's appointments, trying to keep an eye on the reception area for Cynthia, who had ducked into the bathroom. When the phone rang, I dashed out into the hall and grabbed the extension. The sound of his voice made me smile.

"Hello, Samantha," he said cheerfully. "I'll bet you thought I'd forgotten all about our dinner date tonight, didn't you?"

"Well, now that you mention it—" I started.

He didn't wait for me to finish. "This week has been hellacious. Every time I thought about you—which, by the way, was embarrassingly often—I was on my way to interview some robbery victim or standing around with a dozen other reporters at police headquarters waiting for the usual meaningless press release. Not the best environment for making personal phone calls, I can assure you." He paused, probably to breathe, since he'd been talking non-stop, as if the perfunctory press release was about to make an appearance, and he'd have to suddenly hang up.

I wondered what he ate for breakfast. Whatever it was, I could certainly use some of it. "I'm just glad you finally reached me," I said quickly, afraid I might not get a second chance.

"So where would you like to go for dinner?" he asked. "I know this terrific little seafood place right on the beach that serves the most wonderful lobster curry. What do you think? Lobster?"

"Lobster sounds wonderful," I said.

"Or maybe you'd prefer something else? Duck, perhaps. Or beef Wellington."

I couldn't stand it anymore. "Stop! You're torturing me." I laughed. "We missed lunch, again, and I'm starving."

"All the better. So, what'll it be? Your choice."

I suddenly realized that Dr. Augustin had come into the lab from his office and was standing in the doorway, inspecting his fingernails. "I think I'd like seafood," I told Michael, eyeing Dr. Augustin. "What time?"

"Say I pick you up about seven. Or is that too early?" I started to tell him seven was probably a little optimistic, considering it was Friday, but he continued, unabated. "By the way, where do you call home? I assume you don't live there at the hospital."

I chuckled. Sometimes I wondered. "Seven o'clock would be fine," I said, and gave him the address. I glanced over at Dr. Augustin. He had a faint glimmer of a smile on his face. He was feigning interest in one of P.J.'s lab-equipment catalogs, his fingernails apparently having passed muster.

"Great!" he exclaimed. "See you at seven." And before I could respond, he hung up.

"Bye," I said to the receiver. I felt like I'd been worked over by an insurance salesman.

Dr. Augustin came across to my side of the hall and looked down at me, amusement softening his normally sharp features. "Hot date tonight?" he asked.

"A date, yes. I don't know about the 'hot' part." I was

irritated at him, but I didn't know why, exactly. Was I embarrassed? Surely not.

"And who's the lucky guy?"

"You don't know him," I said. "Michael Halsey. I met him last week, here at the clinic." As if it was any of your business, I almost added.

The smile vanished. "Samantha, he's a *reporter,* for God's sake!" He almost choked on the word *reporter*. "And a nosy one at that."

"Reporters serve a very useful purpose," I countered.

"Yeah, so do vultures and sharks." Although only two inches taller than I, he seemed to be towering over me right at that moment. "And he's almost fifty years old!" he added.

I scowled at him. "How did you know that?" I asked.

He looked smug. Disgustingly so. "I have ears. Or haven't any of you around here figured that out yet?"

I could feel my face redden. Damn him. I smiled suddenly. Smiling had always been my best weapon. "So what? You're almost fifty." I poked his rock-hard stomach with my finger.

"Not for another ten years, I'm not. A whole decade!" He had his arms folded across his chest, and he looked kind of cute leaning against the wall, face flushed, eyes stormy.

"And he's in great shape for almost fifty," I said, teasing him. "Anyway, why are you so concerned about who I date? What business is it of yours?" I knew as soon as the question was out, I shouldn't have asked it.

He looked momentarily at a loss. "I just don't want anyone who works for me to get into trouble," he said finally. "And that guy looks like trouble."

Suddenly I wasn't amused anymore. "For crying out loud, I'm only going to dinner with him."

We were staring hard at each other there in the hallway,

our eyes duking it out like silent warriors—blue against black, and black was winning. I looked away. I heard him exhale a blast of air.

"Oh, all right," he said, "have it your way. Date anyone you like. This is wasting time, and we have clients to see."

I looked up, my mouth set to fire another volley, but he was already heading into his office. At that moment P.J. and Cynthia stuck their faces around the corner, grinning like a couple of idiots.

"Shut up," I snapped and went back into Room 2. By God, I thought, I am going to punch out at 5:30, if it kills me.

At 5:15, with both exam rooms full and two more clients waiting in the wings, I began calculating exactly how long it would take me to shower and dress. I could probably make it, if I left by 6:20, I told myself as I headed into Room 1.

The Ames cat was lying on the table, his left ear, or what remained of it, slowly weeping tiny globules of blood and grunge onto the cuff of Mr. Ames's white dress shirt. It was fortunate Mrs. Ames and their five children had remained at home, because Dr. Augustin did not look like he was in the mood to be particularly civil.

I gently pried Bruiser away from Mr. Ames and took hold of his front feet and head so that Dr. Augustin could safely examine the tattered ear. Bruiser, however, didn't seem to mind.

Dr. Augustin wiped at the ear with a gauze sponge. He glanced over at Mr. Ames. "One of these days Bruiser is going to get sick from a bite wound like this, and we're not going to be able to save him. There are diseases out there, Mr. Ames, for which there are no cures or vaccines." He reached for the bottle of surgical scrub soap. "As I have told you before, neutering would help stop him from wandering around the neighborhood looking for trouble."

And females in heat, I wanted him to say, but this time he avoided the subject of birth control entirely. I figured he probably felt it was pointless, considering the ever-burgeoning Ames family.

"Keeping him inside would be even better," he added instead.

I watched Mr. Ames puff out his chest and raise his chin. He was a tall, wiry man, somewhere between twenty-five and thirty years of age, with very curly red hair and a full beard that needed trimming. He was always dressed in a suit and tie, the few times that I had seen him, but, like Dr. Augustin, would have looked more natural in jeans and a work shirt.

"We have been over this before," he growled in response. "I am paying you to fix my cat's ear, not lecture me."

I was surprised he didn't ask Dr. Augustin how *he* would feel if someone decided to castrate *him*. For some reason, they were both avoiding the subject of reproduction like a couple of Victorian spinsters.

"A more worthwhile endeavor would be to help us shut down that greyhound track."

I felt my mouth drop open, and I looked quickly at Dr. Augustin. Outwardly, he was still intent on Bruiser's ear. Had he been a cat, I'm sure his hair would have stood on end, and he would have arched his back and flattened his ears. His face was telling me to duck. Of course, you had to know Dr. Augustin pretty well to read him, and Mr. Ames didn't, so he continued.

"It's barbaric the way those poor dogs are treated. Kept all of their lives in tiny metal cages hardly big enough to stand up in. Made to run day in and day out after some mechanical rabbit so drug addicts and drunks can gamble welfare money on them." He paused. "The lucky ones are the losers. And the dogs that refuse to run at all. They're put out of their misery. By the thousands, I might add."

Dr. Augustin looked up at Mr. Ames with his blackest stare, but Mr. Ames didn't seem to notice.

"The way they're treated, I'm surprised they haven't attacked and killed more people than they have. I'm just thankful it wasn't my daughter who was maimed last week."

Having said his piece, Mr. Ames pulled his lips thinly together and looked down his nose at us. Dr. Augustin gathered up the dirty sponges and threw them into the trash. Then he began to wash his hands, his back to Mr. Ames. He didn't say anything for a few seconds. When he turned around, his face was calm.

"The bleeding has stopped," he told Mr. Ames, "but I think we should keep Bruiser overnight for observation. He'll need medication, and we may need to close up that ear, after all, especially if he worries it."

Mr. Ames relaxed his shoulders and, for a moment, I thought he was going to smile. He seemed relieved that Dr. Augustin hadn't taken up the gauntlet, after all. "All right," he said. "I'll have Louisa come by for him tomorrow." He gave Bruiser a farewell pat and left, without saying thank you, or good-bye, or anything. At least he didn't pursue the greyhound issue, I thought.

Dr. Augustin lifted Bruiser off the table and carried him into Isolation. Joker stood up in his cage, tail wagging expectantly, tongue lolling. I tried to imagine Rachel's dogs as unfortunate, abused creatures in need of a savior like Mr. Ames, but couldn't, no matter how hard I tried.

"What seems to be Mr. Ames's problem?" I asked as I filled a disposable litter pan.

Dr. Augustin was writing something on Bruiser's cage card. "He thinks he's an animal-rights advocate. In reality, he does more harm than good. Half the time he doesn't know what he's talking about or tells only part of the story. Even when he does have the facts, he rants and raves like a fanatic, and no one of any consequence listens to him. He'd be dangerous, if he wasn't so obviously Looney Tunes all the time."

I put a dish of water in Bruiser's cage. "Who is this *us* he was talking about?"

Dr. Augustin shrugged. "Who knows? Probably just him and his wife. No intelligent person bent on protecting the rights of animals would want to associate with him. In any case, we obviously are not going to change their minds about anything, poor Bruiser included." Bruiser's good ear perked up at the sound of his name. "I don't know why I keep trying."

He sighed, and I followed him across the hall to Room 2. It was 5:40. I decided it was going to take a miracle to get me out of there in thirty minutes and began praying.

CHAPTER 10

•

The doorbell rang precisely at seven o'clock. The sound startled me. Tina hopped off the bathroom countertop and slithered across the floor to my bed. For a second I seriously considered joining her there in the darkness, amid the gremlins and dust bunnies. I'd been home all of twenty minutes and felt like I'd thrown myself together without a plan.

I stared at my image in the mirror. I was wearing a teal, drop-waist knit dress with matching earrings and gray pumps, and the strange, yet ostensibly chic silver bracelet a friend had given me for Christmas. My mother would approve, I thought. She had bought the dress for me on a whim a couple of years before, because I liked the color, and because it made me look taller and thinner. Not that I needed to look taller, but where I came from, one could never be too thin. It had cost a fortune. I suspected she had also bought it because she'd wanted me to have something nice—no, something expensive—in case I changed my mind about men.

I tossed the unused tube of lipstick back in the drawer. "Enough is enough," I said out loud as the doorbell rang again. "Let's not get carried away."

I went to the door, swallowing my anxiety. I'd forgotten

what it was like to play the dating game. It had been so long ago. At least it seemed that way. And then I smiled when I opened the door, because despite his almost fifty years, Michael looked like a nervous teenager standing there on the landing, hair freshly washed and still damp, shirt collar squeezing his Adam's apple.

"Hello, Michael," I said.

He was wearing his essence of forest. It seemed somehow less appropriate with his gray, pin-striped suit and conservative tie than it had with the polo shirt and deck shoes.

"You look lovely, Samantha," he said. "I hardly recognized you." He blushed, then went on hastily. "What I meant was, the uniform doesn't do you justice."

I laughed, finding suddenly that I'd relaxed. "Thank you," I said. "Would you like a glass of wine?" It was all I had, but it wasn't a bad wine. I had purposely hidden it from Jeffrey, who didn't know a chardonnay from a zinfandel.

"I'd love a glass, but I really think we should be going. Our reservation is for seven-thirty."

He was studying my apartment, his eyes traveling over each wall and each piece of furniture inquiringly, as if searching for something. I couldn't tell what he was thinking, and he was making me nervous again.

I picked up my purse. "I'm ready," I said.

Tuttles is a small, unpretentious building nestled among the sea oats in a very exclusive part of Cortez Point, five miles south of Brightwater Beach. It is perched on stilts and covered with weathered cypress and rough-cut, gray shingles. At one time it was a private beach residence, but now sports a wide circular drive and a small porous-pavement parking lot. I had passed it a hundred times and never really paid much attention to it before then.

An inconspicuous sign reads, TUTTLES ON THE BEACH. FINE SEAFOOD. RESERVATIONS SUGGESTED. There are no rusting anchors or coils of rope, no fake portholes or pieces of plastic coral cluttering the exterior. Nothing to attract the tourists who want to experience the "Real Florida," but who, at lesser establishments, often wind up eating frozen Atlantic cod masquerading as grouper or red snapper.

Michael dropped me off at the door and went to park his BMW alongside the Mercedes and Lincolns already decorating the pavement. A young man, appropriately attired in black and white, sat on a stool by a portable sign that read VALET PARKING, looking bored. The parking lot is close enough to the building that I doubted many people took advantage of his services. Times were tough, even for the rich. Which, I realized now, included Michael Halsey, at least to some extent. And I wondered how he managed to qualify on a reporter's salary. Maybe he hustles rich women, I thought, chuckling to myself, and he's checking out my portfolio.

I waited under the awning but stood far enough away from the door that the valet wouldn't feel obligated to open it for me. He was kind of cute, in a Beach Boys sort of way. I imagined that he spent his days tending bar in one of those little open-air oases that dot the sand like flotsam after a storm, where they serve grouper sandwiches and play Jimmy Buffett's "Marguerritaville" over and over on the jukebox. Everyone always looks the same age in those places, because once your skin gets tan enough, it turns to leather.

I had spent my share of weekends in one or two beach bars, especially after fleeing the pompousness of the north. I'd eat u-peel-em shrimp and suck Corona beer through a section of lime stuffed down the neck of the bottle, because that's the way everyone drank it. At beach bars, you can't tell the doctors and lawyers and corporate executives from the ordinary people, not with only six inches of spandex covering the appropriate areas.

I went there, because after a few beers and a few turns of "Margueritaville" I could pretend I was anybody I wanted, and the guy I was talking to was anybody I wanted him to be. Like everyone who goes to those places, I went there to escape. The problem was, reality came slinking back on Monday morning with its tail between its legs, and after a while I gave up trying to escape and decided to make the most of what reality had to offer. So, here I was in my Sunday best trying to remember if a California chardonnay went better with lobster than a gewürztraminer.

Michael put his hand on my shoulder. I jumped, and he snatched his hand away like I'd been a tree branch that had suddenly turned into a water moccasin.

"Sorry," I said. "I was daydreaming."

He smiled, relieved, I supposed, that my reaction hadn't been because he had dared touch me. "Think nothing of it. I've been guilty of the same thing, myself, on occasion." He motioned toward the door. "After you."

The valet, eager to be doing *anything,* even for free, hopped off his perch and opened the door. He winked at me, and I said, "Thank you," and smiled as seductively as I could, so his evening wouldn't be a complete waste.

You had to step up to the reservation desk, which was located on a carpeted platform of sorts, where the maître d' stood amid a jungle of dieffenbachia and ficus and looked out over the dining room like a sheep dog guarding his flock. Everything was done in shades of aqua and coral and white, with chrome-and-glass accents. Huge potted plants sat here and there, waiting to grab at you as you walked by—giant photosynthetic monsters from some Japanese sci-fi movie. But the most noticeable feature of the room was the west wall, which was an enormous picture window, floor to ceiling, that looked out over the beach and the Gulf of Mexico.

The sun had set an hour before. Now the moon hung in the sky like one of those star-spangled orbs they have in ballrooms, casting a shower of diamonds across the water, making the beach look like snow. It was spectacular, and I felt that if the chef wanted to serve Atlantic cod flown in frozen from New York, he could, and no one would notice.

The maître d' picked up a couple of menus and led us across the plush carpeting to a table for two right next to the window. He pulled out my chair and, after I'd settled in it, opened up my napkin for me. I continued to gaze out at the silver sea and the tiny windup birds that, despite the late hour, continued to dash up and down the beach, bobbing for coquinas.

Surprisingly, the noise level in the nearly full dining room was low. Quiet laughter, the occasional tinkle of crystal, and the sounds of cutlery against fine china did little to interfere with the strains of Vivaldi that floated airily across the room from somewhere near the foyer. I was tired, and the music and the beach calmed me. I felt like I was floating in a warm pool in the dark—a sort of sensory-deprivation chamber—and I didn't hear Michael right away.

"Samantha," he was saying. "Earth to Samantha." I turned my head and smiled apologetically.

"The beach is so incredibly beautiful—I got caught up in it." He is going to think I'm a bubble brain, I thought morosely. At the very least, he's going to think I'm not interested in him.

"Would you like something to drink?" he asked, apparently for the second time.

Our waiter, who could have passed for Jeffrey's twin, except for his expression, which was far from angelic, was standing beside the table. He had that "I'm only here until I get the result of my bar exam" look waiters at very expensive restaurants often get. Like three hundred bucks a night was chicken feed compared with what he was planning on making.

I wanted a beer but ordered a Jack Daniel's and water instead. It would be more socially acceptable and would keep me from drinking too much, since I was not particularly fond of liquor. Michael ordered a Scotch and soda, which didn't really surprise me.

I opened my menu. "Do you come here often?" I asked him, not looking up. He was watching me, and I wasn't prepared yet to watch him back.

"Now and then," he answered. "Not as often as I used to . . ." His voice trailed off, and when I reluctantly shifted my gaze from the appetizers, I saw that he was staring out the window, a look of profound sadness reflecting back from the glass. "My wife, Mary, and I used to come here all of the time." He paused, as if unsure about continuing. "She died two years ago."

His words made me flinch. I reached out, and before I knew what I was doing, I put my hand over his. "I'm so very sorry, Michael," I said.

He turned from the window and took my hand in his, then slowly smiled. He had a pleasant face, with nice, even features and just the hint of a cleft in his chin. But his eyes—there was something about his eyes that bothered me. Something about the way he was staring at me. Suddenly I wanted to ask him what his wife had looked like. What color hair she had had.

I withdrew my hand as nonchalantly as possible, grateful

that our drinks had arrived. I took a sip and picked up my menu. Michael opened his, obviously thankful for the interruption as well. I wondered with amusement how men and women feeling each other out, metaphorically speaking, would be able to cope if there weren't any menus to hold and read and make polite conversation over.

We discussed the selections and, on the advice of Jeffrey's twin, who had seen fit to share some of his inestimable knowledge (and his time) with us, ordered angels on horseback and a bottle of gewürztraminer. While we waited we talked about our favorite foods and the restaurants we'd visited, his list of course being longer and more prestigious than mine.

After the oysters arrived, and as I was contentedly munching on one, noticing how fresh they were and how the bacon wasn't too crisp, I tried to tell myself it didn't really matter. That u-peel-um shrimp and a beer at the Oasis were just as good as a meal at Tuttles any day. Of course, that was a little like trying to tell Miss Priss that her low-cal, dry cat food was just as good as Chicken of the Sea.

"So, how long have you lived in Florida?" Michael asked me, reaching across the table to fill my wineglass. "From that faint trace of New England in your voice, I have to assume you weren't born here." He was once again smiling playfully, the sadness gone from his face, as if I had only imagined it.

"Almost three years," I said. "I came here a couple of times on spring break and fell in love with the beach . . . the white sand and warm water. Anyway, I decided the first chance I got, I'd move here." I made a production of scooping up another oyster. It wasn't really a lie. I *had* spent Easter vacation in Ft. Lauderdale my sophomore year. And I *had* liked the beach. Not enough to leave Connecticut, though. Not then, anyway. "And what brought you to the Sunshine State?" I asked hastily.

Michael regarded me for a moment, then shrugged. "I came for the fishing, mostly. And the climate. I've never been one for snow. I'd rather be out on my boat fighting a marlin than on some ski slope breaking my neck."

"You have a boat?" I put down my fork.

Michael saw the flicker of interest and grinned. "Yes," he said. "A forty-footer, named the *Serendipity*. It's moored over at the Brightwater Beach Marina."

Before I had a chance to comment, our waiter, who obviously had plans for later that evening, insisted that we order. I chose coquilles St. Jacques, and Michael went for the lobster curry with mango chutney. My untouched cocktail was still sitting next to my water glass, and Michael didn't pressure me into sharing a second bottle of wine, although he offered. I reminded him I had to work the next day.

The salads came, and I quickly resumed our earlier discussion. "How do you find the time to go out in your boat?" I asked, pushing a cherry tomato around on my plate. Covered with creamy dill dressing, it eluded my knife and fork like a greased pig. "You can't just hop in a forty-foot boat for a quick spin around the bay, can you?" I gave the tomato a reprieve and speared a cucumber slice instead.

"No, not really," he conceded. "But I manage to take her out once or twice a month. And for two weeks each year, I take her down to Bimini or St. Thomas. Mostly, I just sit on her deck there at the dock and relax." He smiled. "Or take out my frustrations polishing her fittings." He poured wine into our glasses. "You should, as they say, come up and see me sometime." The smile had turned into a roguish grin, which, like the aftershave, seemed out of character. Maybe it was the oysters. "I'll even fix you dinner. I'm a pretty fair cook, if I *do* say so." It was hard to tell if the light from the candle on the table was playing tricks, or if there was a gleam in his eye.

"Have you always owned a boat?" I asked, pointedly ignoring the invitation.

"Do toy boats count?"

I laughed, and then Michael's attention was diverted by the arrival of the main course. Service may not be the house specialty, I thought as I admired my plate, but even the *Times* food critic couldn't fault the presentation.

"This looks wonderful," I said, and Michael agreed, and the conversation turned to the joys of fresh seafood and life, generally, in Paradise. The gleam in his eye, if indeed there had been one, was gone.

When our waiter saw that most of his assigned tables were nearing the end of their meals, he began circling the room like some vulture eyeing a fresh road kill. His eagerness to see us out of there so that he could collect his twenty percent and move on to the next round irritated Michael, and he decided to order dessert, even though we'd both agreed we wouldn't.

The thought of putting another morsel of food or drop of liquid into my mouth, much less into my stomach, appalled me.

"Try the baked custard with caramel sauce, Samantha," Michael suggested, leaning back in his chair. "It's very good and not too filling." Before I could object, he had ordered some for both of us, and coffee. The vulture looked down his beak at Michael, but went back to the kitchen without so much as a peep.

I swallowed forcefully. "I'll have to eat low-fat cottage

cheese and carrot sticks for a month after tonight," I said with a weak grin.

Michael laughed. "You worry too much about your weight," he told me. "You look fine just the way you are." He was watching me again, that same wistful expression on his face he'd had earlier.

I desperately needed a change of subject. "Whatever made you decide to become a *reporter*?" I asked, sorry it had come out sounding like Dr. Augustin had asked the question.

"It has its moments," he said. "And it keeps me out of trouble."

When he didn't elaborate, I quickly picked it up. "Just what kind of trouble are you likely to get into?"

He chuckled. "Oh, knocking off liquor stores, snatching little old ladies' purses. Running for governor. That sort of thing."

Michael was carefully avoiding any mention of his wife, as if his earlier disclosure was an accident, a memory that had surfaced and slipped out when he wasn't looking. Except for one fleeting moment, neither of us had divulged even as much information as an ordinary obituary in the *Times* might contain.

Our waiter flapped over to our table and all but flung the dessert dishes and coffee cups at us, then flapped off again in search of easier prey. I saw that Michael had taken careful note, his lips pulled back in a sort of grimace, not unlike the expression a dog gets when it smells blood. I wondered how much tip our legal eagle thought he was going to receive acting like a spoiled brat. If he was planning on paying off his law-school loan with what he garnered at Tuttles, he probably should make other arrangements. According to the small print on the menu, the gratuity would not be included in the bill, and I felt certain if Michael had his way, it would not be included in our payment, either.

Michael looked over at me and smirked. "So whatever made you decide to be a veterinary nurse?" he asked, adding cream to his coffee.

"Technician," I corrected gently. "Same thing, different title."

"Sorry. Technician."

"My father was . . . is . . . a surgeon," I said flatly. "I guess medicine is in my blood." I smiled. "Unfortunately, I never really liked school until halfway through college. By then, it was too late." I put a small spoonful of custard in my mouth and swallowed. It wasn't too bad. "So I got a degree in veterinary technology and went to work in a research lab."

I looked out of the window at a couple walking along the sea edge, hand in hand, their silhouettes joined like paper dolls. "It was really depressing, caring for all those animals, week after week, only to walk in one morning and find the whole lot of them had been sacrificed the night before by one of the researchers. I just couldn't handle it. No matter *how* important the experiments were." I turned back to Michael and shrugged. "I guess I'd have made a pretty lousy doctor. Too emotional."

Michael reached across the table and took my hand. I didn't resist. "Don't put yourself down, Samantha," he said quietly, in a firm, yet gentle tone of voice. "I have a feeling you'd be successful at almost anything you tried, once you put your mind to it." He rubbed his thumb idly across the top of my hand, as one might investigate the texture of a piece of fabric. It appeared to be an unconscious movement that I found mildly relaxing. "Not to change the subject, but how is that dog doing—the one from the greyhound track?"

I sat up, pulling back my hand. He made no move to recapture it, and I was no longer inclined to let him, anyway. The spell was broken.

The eagle drew in his wings and dove through the air, landing at our table with the bill on a small silver tray. No "Would you like more coffee?" or "How was your meal?" He stood waiting, glaring down at Michael with beady eyes, talons ready to grab up the payment and fly off. Michael took out his wallet, carefully extracted several bills, counted them ever so slowly, then placed them on the tray.

The eagle, who had counted the bills right along with Michael, continued to stand by the table, his hands on his hips, eyes growing beadier by the minute. Michael stood up and moved around the table to help me with my chair, almost as if the young man was already a memory. It was a duel to the death, and my money was on my date.

I picked up my purse, and we headed for the door, leaving the eagle to contemplate the contents of the salver, like his prey had turned out to be nothing more than a bag of bones, no meat anywhere.

"How much did you leave him, if I may ask?" I whispered, after we had passed by the maître d'.

"Enough so he'd realize it wasn't an oversight," he said, with obvious satisfaction.

I grinned at him. One thing was sure. This man had style. But, I mused, after nearly two and a half hours alone with the guy, you'd have thought I would discover a bit more about him than the fact that he was a widower whose favorite boats were Cutty Sark and Chris-Craft.

Michael opened the fashionably stark door, offered me his arm, and together we stepped out into the kind of night you read about in Danielle Steel novels.

CHAPTER 11

•

Saturday, February 19

Dr. Augustin appeared in the doorway to Room 2 looking faintly amused. "Been putting on a few pounds, have we?"

I hopped off the scale, quickly sucking in my stomach. "Just keeping track of my weight," I said. I'd gained almost five pounds since early December, and my date with Michael was sure to add a few more. Unfortunately, even as a teenager, purging had never appealed to me.

"I guess P.J.'s not coming in today," he said. "I didn't even know she was sick." I didn't say anything. "So, I'm afraid you'll have to do double duty. I promise to go easy on you." Again, the faint look of amusement.

He didn't ask me about my date, didn't say "Good morning." Something's up, I thought. He stood in the doorway, like he wanted to say something but couldn't figure out how to go about it.

I took out a fresh roll of paper towels from under the sink. "Thanks," I said. "I'll try not to put us too far behind."

"Sam . . . I've got a favor to ask of you." He rocked gently back and forth on his heels, as if working out a cramp.

"What's that?"

"Rachel's house was broken into last night," he said. "They ransacked the place, but didn't take anything. I figure it has to do with the threats she's been getting. She saw one of the track people drive away in a big hurry. Harvey Snead, I think she said, or Stead. A leadout." He drew a deep breath.

"The point is I don't want her staying there by herself, until the police find the guy. She won't go to a motel. Says she can't afford it." He paused. "Would it be okay if she stayed with you for the weekend? At least until Monday. You . . . don't . . . have any plans . . . do you?"

He seemed embarrassed, and I realized he meant the possibility that someone—a man—might be staying there with me. He really knew very little about me. Very little of a personal nature, at any rate. Of course, I really knew very little about *his* personal life, either—who he dated, if anyone, where he spent his free time. He worked out at a health club somewhere in town and went backpacking in Montana for two weeks every summer. I knew that much. We'd been out for a couple of beers on two or three occasions, but always with a group. And he always came by himself.

"No," I answered, "no plans."

He looked relieved. "Well—would you mind?" he asked. "I'll even do treatments for you Sunday."

What was I going to say, "Of course I mind having your ex wife stay with me"? "No, I guess not. I'll borrow a rollaway from my landlord." We went into the lab. "I hope she likes cats."

"Sure, Rachel is a sucker for anything with four legs." He smiled. Like we were just having a casual chat on a typical Saturday morning in Paradise.

"It's the two-legged variety she has trouble with, is that it?" I asked, smirking. My tongue had developed a mind of its own.

A dark shadow passed over his face, and I expected a bolt of lightning to strike me dead on the spot. "She'll be over tonight after the last race," he said curtly, then turned around and left, shoulders squared, chin up.

Things got really busy about three, and Dr. Augustin called Frank up from the kennel to help. I was furious. Not only had I failed to be in two places at once, but now I had to put up with the kennel Casanova.

Of course, I said nothing, and Frank spent the next two hours strutting around like he was on stage somewhere, performing. I left at six and headed for the Rose and Crown. For once, I was not looking forward to the rest of the weekend.

Rachel put her duffel bag on the rollaway and looked around. "This is very nice," she said in that tone of voice people use when they don't know what else to say, but feel they should say *something*. "I like the color of these walls. Peach, isn't it?"

"Apricot blush, actually," I said. "I call it my womb color. Good for sleep, according to the man at the paint store." I got out a clean towel and washcloth from my closet and handed them to Rachel. "I hope you don't mind sharing my bedroom," I said.

"Not at all. It's very nice of you to put me up. Especially under the circumstances."

Did I really have a choice? I asked myself. Then I noticed how small and vulnerable she looked, standing there in the corner in an enormous sweater that might have belonged to a man twice her size, might even have been one of Dr. Augustin's. She had her hands jammed in the pockets of her denim skirt, as if trying to control them, as if they might take off on their own. Tiny wisps of hair protruded from what I felt certain had once been a neat French braid. Her face was pale. It was almost like she had been roused from her bed and forced to make a hasty exit in the middle of the night.

Suddenly I felt sorry for her. She didn't ask to have her privacy invaded. She didn't deserve what was happening to her. She certainly didn't deserve to be treated like a leper.

"You must be exhausted," I said. I looked at the clock next to my bed. "It's nearly midnight. Maybe we should turn in."

She shook her head. "I'm really not sleepy yet." She was fiddling with her duffel bag. "I need a little time to unwind. You go on to bed, Samantha." She held up a dog-eared paperback. "A couple of chapters should do the trick."

"I'm not sleepy yet, either. How about some herbal tea?" I paused for a moment, and she nodded, smiling

"Thank you, that would be nice." She followed me into the kitchen.

"How long do you think it will be before they catch this Snead guy?" I asked as I filled my teapot.

"I'm not sure. He knows I spotted him, so he'd be an idiot to go back to the track."

We went into the living room and sat down—Rachel on the sofa and me on my father's old recliner. Miss Priss sauntered into the room, hopped up on the sofa, and slowly eased herself into Rachel's lap. Rachel knew all the right places to scratch, and Miss Priss smiled at me, her eyes closed to slits, her front paws gently kneading imaginary milk out of Rachel's left leg. Her throaty rumble reminded me of a jet engine droning away in the distance.

Rachel grinned. "I've got two cats of my own," she said. Then she frowned. "Russell promised to check on them when he goes out to my place to feed the dogs. I've got a pregnant bitch staying there, and two others recovering from injuries. I hate to leave them alone overnight, but Lou is dead set against me going back to the house." She grinned suddenly. "You know how he is."

Indeed, I thought. "How did you get involved in greyhound racing, anyway?" I asked.

"My father was an engineer with Tampa Electric. When my grandfather died and left Dad the farmhouse and one hundred acres of dead orange trees, he decided to take an early retirement and move out there. Mom and I weren't too keen about living so far from downtown Tampa—not that it's all that far now—but what could we do?

"He wanted to raise dogs for the pet industry—good dogs, from good parents, properly cared for and socialized. When I was a kid, he got me a German shepherd puppy. A beautiful dog, with a pedigree as long as your arm. Longer. Or so he thought. She'd inherited hip dysplasia from the father, apparently. It was so bad, we had to have her put down before her fourth birthday."

She smiled at Priss, who was napping, her head draped over Rachel's left knee, her backside sliding off the right one. I really must put her on a diet, I thought absently.

"First it was golden retrievers. Then, at a dog show in Orlando, he met up with Barry Labeau, one of the kennel owners over at Suncoast. Before Mom and I knew what had happened, Dad had sunk every cent of his savings into greyhounds. Hired himself a trainer, got a kennelful of dogs, finagled a lease out of Suncoast . . . the whole show."

A shrill whistling began suddenly in the kitchen, startling Rachel. Priss cracked an amber eye and flicked the last two joints of her tail to indicate her resentment at being jostled, but did not budge.

"Go on," I told Rachel as I got up and went for our tea.

"That was twenty years ago." She paused, then continued, her voice hinting sadness. "Mom died in eighty-six, and my dad never got over it. He had a heart attack two years later."

I carried the tea in on a tray. Rachel gently lifted Priss from her lap and placed the comatose body next to her on the sofa.

"I moved back in with Dad after the funeral. He needed my help with the financial end of the business." She smiled. "I was working as an accountant in St. Petersburg. For a man I nearly married. It was probably for the best—my leaving. He really wasn't particularly good for me."

She stirred a little sugar into her tea, and then I lost her as she sailed down some tributary memory. It was a brief trip.

"When Dad died, I thought about selling the place, dogs and all. Land prices, especially that close to the interstate, had gone way up. It was tempting, to say the least."

"What made you change your mind?"

"It's hard. You get so attached. . . ." Her eyes began to glisten, and she looked away. I figured she was thinking about Magic and R.C. She took a deep breath and then a sip of tea, regaining her composure in time.

"I decided to try my hand at running a kennel." She chuckled, but she didn't look amused. "I was doing pretty well, too, until recently. Even won the Summerland Stake last year with R.C." She began stroking Priss again.

"Where did you meet Dr. Augustin?" I asked, trying not to appear too interested. Like we were still engaging in small talk.

She looked up and grinned. "I had been taking my cats to Dr. Early, over at Pine Bluffs Animal Hospital. When he decided to retire and sell his property to some condo developer, he suggested I try the new vet here in Paradise

Cay, even though it was out of my way. He said he'd heard good things about the guy. I think old Dr. Early had a little matchmaker in him, if you want *my* opinion."

She kicked off her shoes, leaned back, and pulled her feet up under her. I glanced down at her shoes—black leather lace-ups that were so small they looked like doll's shoes.

"Lou was one of the most attractive men I had ever met," she went on. "He swept me off my feet, no doubt about it."

Her eyes met mine. I drained the last of my tea and slowly put my cup down on the coffee table, noticing the faint water rings and tiny scratches that my mother said added character to an antique. I had heard her say the same thing about wrinkles and gray hair.

"It just didn't work out," she announced, after an uncomfortable silence.

I looked up at her, hoping she would elaborate without any prompting from me. It really wasn't any of my business, after all. But Rachel was obviously in a talkative mood.

"I got tired of being 'protected' all the time," she said, and I noticed a touch of bitterness in her voice. "Like I couldn't take care of myself. Like I was some pampered poodle or something. I have that effect on men, and it infuriates me." I didn't say anything, and her expression softened. "It isn't that Lou doesn't mean well. Under all that machismo, he's really a very nice person. Faithful, caring. But he didn't *need* me, and I just couldn't live with that."

Suddenly I realized Rachel still loved him, probably more than he loved her. But I also believed she would never allow him back into her life. And I wasn't sure how I felt about that. I was growing fond of Rachel.

Suddenly Tina appeared out of nowhere and began making her way cautiously to the front door, her eyes darting periodically back to Rachel.

"That must be Jeffrey, my next-door neighbor," I said, and got up. "He usually stops by on his way home from work with leftovers for the cats." I laughed. "Don't tell Dr. Augustin, or I'll never hear the end of it. Veterinary technicians are supposed to know better."

Miss Priss, suddenly aware that food might be in the offing, oozed off the sofa, hitting the floor with a thud. She ambled over to take up a position next to Tina.

I opened the door before Jeff could free up a hand. "Come in," I said. "Your fan club awaits you."

Jeffrey smiled his marvelous smile and came in, his arms full of carryout boxes and a brown paper sack whose contents rattled suspiciously like beer bottles. It must be payday, I thought. Once in the kitchen, Jeff began unloading his presents. The irresistible odor of beef in some kind of wine sauce crept out of one of the Styrofoam containers. My cats began dancing around on their toenails and crying pitiful sounds of starvation.

"You should feed these poor creatures occasionally, Sam," Jeffrey said with a grin.

I glared at him.

He continued. "I brought enough of this beef burgundy stuff for an army." He began fumbling about in my catchall drawer for a bottle opener. "I figured you might like a little midnight snack." He took the tops off two bottles of Heineken and inclined his head toward the living room. "Would your guest want one?" he asked.

"Probably," I said, and Jeff opened a third bottle.

After I'd made the introductions and the five of us had eaten our fill of beef burgundy on rice with broccoli au gratin, and the beer was almost gone, I brought up the subject of the boycott and the threats.

"This Snead person—do you think he's the one who's been drugging your dogs?" I asked.

She glanced over at Jeffrey, who had fallen asleep in my recliner. Rachel and I were curled up on opposite ends of the sofa.

"Oh, don't worry about him," I told her quickly. "Even if he overheard us, he wouldn't repeat it outside of this apartment."

She didn't look convinced and answered me in an almost whisper. "As a leadout, Harvey certainly would have an opportunity, but he's not bright enough to be doing it on his own and really has nothing to gain, unless he's trying to fix races. No . . . I'm sure he's working for Donovan."

"You've spoken to Donovan?"

"I don't know if *spoken* is the right word." She wrapped her arms around her knees and hugged tight, her eyes fixed on the far wall. "Screamed is more like it." She smiled somewhat sardonically.

"Oh, we started out being more or less civil to one another. He denied threatening me on the phone, but said I deserved whatever I got for trying to ruin a good thing. I guess he and his old cronies don't care what they feed their dogs as long as it's cheap, and over the short term they can't see any difference in performance.

"I'm afraid I lost my temper and accused him of killing R.C.—that I knew he was involved. It was a stupid thing to say, but I was hoping he would confess. Of course, he denied that, too, and called me a lot of ugly names and shoved me out of his kennel. He slammed the door so hard the crates inside rattled. That set off his dogs, and I heard him throw a food dish at one of them."

"What *did* the guy on the phone say to you?" I asked her. "The one who threatened you?"

"He told me to lay off about the food, or something unpleasant might happen. He wasn't specific. Then, after I started talking around about a boycott, I got another call from the same person, telling me I had been warned, and now I would pay. I'm almost positive it was Donovan."

"Did you tell the police about the threats or the drugs?"

Rachel shook her head slowly and looked down at her hands. "No, I didn't." She obviously wasn't going to tell me why.

"How's the boycott coming, anyway?"

Rachel straightened out her legs and stretched. Then she yawned. I looked over at the clock on the VCR. It read 2:45.

"What boycott? I can't even get half of the owners to fight this thing with me. Most of them just don't want to get involved. More than a few, though, are just like Donovan. Good ol' boys who don't give a damn about the dogs, as long as they perform. They're too stupid to realize that if you treat the animals with respect and care for them properly, they'll run their hearts out for you. Greyhounds love to run." She paused. "I'm thinking about going to the health department. Maybe they can look into it.

"You know, I honestly thought I had done some good, asking Tom Rheems for help. The meat I received the following week wasn't too bad. Then I found out I was apparently the only one getting it. Everyone else was still being sent the garbage Bayside started delivering last November. Someone was obviously hoping I would shut up, if I thought I had won. Of course, it only made me madder."

Jeffrey stirred, and I decided it was time he went home.

"Come on, Jeffrey, time for bed," I announced from the sofa. Jeff rubbed the back of his neck, flexed his long legs, and stood up.

"If you insist," he said, smiling. "It was nice to meet you,

Mrs. Augustin. I'm sorry about your house and all. I hope the three of us can get together again." He laughed. "Maybe I can stay awake next time." He headed for the door.

Rachel and I got up and went with him. "Thank you for the dinner, Jeff," she said.

"Don't thank me, thank Freddy's," he responded. "*Au revoir.*"

I could hear him unlocking the door to his apartment. "He's really a terrific guy," I said. Rachel looked at me and grinned.

"How old is he?"

"Twenty-four." I chuckled. "Don't worry, I'm not robbing the cradle. Jeff is just a good friend."

Rachel yawned again, and I pointed her in the direction of the bedroom. That time she didn't resist.

CHAPTER 12

•

Sunday, February 20

The smell of fresh coffee awakened me. I crawled out of bed and ambled sleepily into the kitchen. Rachel was buttering an English muffin. She'd managed to shower and dress without waking me, which was nice of her, since it was only seven o'clock. For someone who'd had less than four hours' sleep, she looked amazingly chipper.

"You're up early," I said, smiling. I took a mug out of the drainer and poured myself some coffee.

"I hope you don't mind," Rachel said, holding up a muffin half. "Oh, and I fed your cats. They were quite insistent." She offered me the other half of the muffin, but I declined. "I have to go turn out my dogs," she added. "It's Russell's day off."

"Mind if I tag along?" I asked. "I'd like to see your dogs and the kennel."

Rachel laughed, and I realized I had never heard her do that before. "Lou wants you to keep an eye on me, is that it?"

"Something like that," I admitted. "But I don't have anything else planned. I certainly don't want to stay here and clean my apartment." No, I thought, what I really want to do is go back to bed.

Rachel took a bite of muffin. "I don't know if I can get

you a kennel pass on such short notice," she said. I looked puzzled. "Only people with licenses and special permits can have access to the dogs," she continued. "The kennel area is like a fortress." She put down her coffee cup. "But I'll make a few calls and see what I can do."

She headed for the phone, and I went into the bathroom to take a shower. If they were so concerned about protecting the dogs, I thought, then they'd better stop worrying about people like me and start looking at their own people.

When I came out of the bedroom, Rachel was just hanging up the telephone. "Good news," she said, "you can go with me. Dick Fowley, the security guard at the compound, will have a pass for you when we get there."

"Great, let's do it," I said, hopeful that the fresh air would revive me. I was starting to feel the effects of too little sleep.

We took Rachel's car and headed across the bridge to the mainland. The tidal flats were alive with egrets searching for breakfast and diehard fishermen, already up to the tops of their waders in the chilly water. I watched as an old man expertly cast his net high in the air. It landed in a perfect circle in front of him, then sank out of sight.

Slowly, the mangroves and marsh grass gave way to manicured saint augustine lawns and century-old live oaks, shrouded in Spanish moss. Rachel's little Toyota bounced over the ancient brick road that led us past giant porticoed mansions, overlooking the bay. Then, suddenly, we found ourselves traversing the smooth blacktop of Summerland Boulevard. Traffic was light. At eight, Rachel turned onto the narrow service road that led to the kennel compound.

The almost empty parking lot looked like a vast, stagnant black sea surrounded by gray concrete and metal cliffs. Without the splash of chrome and color from row upon row of parked cars and the excited buzz of the crowds, the entire place, from the front at least, seemed old and dreary.

We took a side road around to the track, ignoring a "Wrong Way—Do Not Enter" sign. The scene there was much improved. The infield lawn was lush and green, despite the winter, and bright, spring annuals had recently been planted around the track's little artificial lake. The lounge and dining areas were encased in several tiers of smoked glass that sparkled in the early-morning sun.

We drove up to the guardhouse at the entrance to what I presumed was the kennel area and stopped. Rachel had been right. The place looked like a military base or prison. Tall, concrete walls, topped with barbed wire, surrounded the entire area. Someone would have to expend a good deal of effort to get in or out without passing by the security guard, who now waved as a pickup truck with an aluminum dog box on top passed through on the side opposite us. Rachel rolled down her window.

"Morning, Dick," she said as the guard opened his door and stepped out. "This is the woman I need the pass for—Samantha Holt. She works for my veterinarian." I leaned forward so he could see me.

"Have it right here, Rachel," he said, handing her a folded-up piece of paper. "Drop it off on your way out, if you don't mind." He went back into his little glass cage, shutting the door behind him. He was about seventy, I decided, with a touch of arthritis—probably a retired policeman who was bored or needed the money.

Rachel stuck the pass under her visor, then drove on through, the little car springing forward like one of her dogs leaving the starting box.

"I told the powers that be you were here to help me treat

a couple of my dogs," she said. "Think of something appropriate, in case we're asked."

I couldn't.

We parked behind a long, low, off-white concrete building, undistinguished except by identical, numbered doors spaced evenly along its exterior. Each door had a coiled-up hose beside it, attached to a water faucet. The building reminded me of the navy barracks I'd seen in Key West sometime back—spartan, monotonous, yet functional, at least from the navy's perspective. I guessed that the dogs, though, probably didn't care what their living quarters looked like.

Rachel unlocked the door marked "6" and led me inside. The door swung closed behind us.

I saw that this "inside" was really "outside," since there were three large, rectangular yards, lined with clean, white sand and enclosed by a six-foot-high fence. There were similar yards on either side of Rachel's and, across the way, more buildings. We passed an ordinary white enamel bathtub propped up on cinder blocks. I caught a whiff of flea dip.

"This is my turnout area," Rachel told me, indicating the pens, "where the dogs can play and relieve themselves."

We heard barking coming from inside the building behind us. Rachel stood quite still for a moment. "Something's wrong," she said. "They usually don't bark like that until the lights have been turned on." She started to put her key in the lock, but the door wasn't closed all the way. It swung open a few inches. She looked at me apprehensively, then slowly pushed it wider.

The barking intensified, and I had to put my hands over my ears. I noticed that the lights were already on. Perhaps she'd forgotten to turn them off and lock up when she left.

Of course, everything I'd learned so far about Rachel told me she would never forget.

We stepped inside, moving almost in slow motion, looking around nervously. I was surprised to see so many dogs in so small a room. There appeared to be about fifty of them, each housed in a roomy, spotlessly clean cage. The name of the dog was taped across the top, and a wire-and-leather muzzle hung from each door. Two rows of cages lined three of the walls, while a U-shaped food-preparation area, consisting of a large chest freezer, a refrigerator, two stainless-steel sinks, and a cupboard occupied the fourth. The freezer's lid apparently doubled as a work surface.

Rachel began checking her dogs, one by one, speaking to them in a calm, even voice, sticking her fingers through the bars for them to lick. Everywhere, tails wagged, and slender bodies jumped and pressed against the wire for attention. One of the cages closest to the kitchen was empty, and the door was unlatched. I peered over the freezer. A man was lying next to the refrigerator.

I knew immediately that the man was dead. His throat had been torn out, and he was lying in a huge puddle of dark, coagulated blood. He looked like some great fish cast up on the beach, half-eaten by the crabs, eyes bulging, mouth agape, his ears sticking out from his head like pectoral fins.

For a moment I thought I was watching one of those slasher movies—*Friday the 13th, Part 20,* or something. I wasn't scared or disgusted, just curious—mesmerized by the Hollywood special effects. Then it hit me. *This* dead person was real. I jumped back away from the freezer and turned around. My face must have been a sight, because Rachel ran over to me and took my hand.

"What's wrong?" she asked, her voice a poor match for the ruckus behind her. My brain was having difficulty communicating with the rest of me, and I didn't answer immediately, so Rachel leaned over the freezer to take a look. When she saw the body, she screamed, then pressed her hand over her mouth. She looked like she was going to be sick, so I quickly steered her toward the door. We both stepped out into the fresh air, and Rachel removed her hand.

"That's Harvey Snead," she managed. "He's the guy I saw driving away from my house Friday night."

"How did he get in here?" I asked.

"I don't know. I distinctly remember locking the door. Besides, he would need a key to get through the outer door—it closes and locks automatically." She paused. "And the guard would have stopped him. No one without a pass is allowed back here except owners and trainers."

She was staring out across the exercise yard. "He probably came here to drug another one of my dogs."

I could hear the emotion, the hostility in her voice, and realized how she must feel, how I felt, about the senselessness of it. "The question is," I said, "what happened to him?"

Suddenly Rachel swung around to face me. I knew from the look in her eyes what she was thinking, and I was surprised it hadn't occurred to us right from the start.

"You don't suppose they'll say I had anything to do with this, do you?" she asked.

Few people would blame her if she did, I thought, but a simple gunshot to the head or a knife through the heart probably would sit better with a jury than ripping the guy's throat out. I didn't say that, of course.

"No, I don't think so," I responded. "But one of your dogs is sure in a lot of trouble."

"What do you mean?" she asked.

"The end cage on the bottom left. The one marked 'Blue Moon.' It's empty."

We looked around the compound for Blue, but she was nowhere to be seen. Rachel had wanted to call the police right away, but I told her Harvey certainly wasn't going anywhere, and Blue might still be hanging around the track. She insisted after a short while, however.

The telephone was in the kitchen area, next to the refrigerator. Rachel stood by the freezer for a few seconds staring at it. There was no way to reach it without stepping in Harvey Snead's blood.

"Let's go ask the guard to call the police," I said.

Rachel appeared relieved. "Good idea," she said.

We walked over to Fowley's little box, and Rachel tapped on the glass. Fowley opened the door.

"There's been an accident," Rachel told him. "A leadout is . . . We found a man in number six. We think he's . . . we think he's dead. Could you call the police?"

Fowley didn't move. He stood in the doorway like a statue, and his face got very white. Then he started to shake. I was afraid we'd soon have two dead people on our hands, but he took a deep breath and slowly nodded. Then he turned to the telephone on his desk.

I took a pen and one of the clinic's business cards out of my purse and wrote Dr. Augustin's home number on it. Then I handed it to Fowley. "And please call Dr. Augustin, too, if you would," I said.

He took the card and began dialing.

The thought that Dr. Augustin might somehow blame me for this latest disaster in Rachel's life occurred to me, but I simply could not think of anyone else to call. Rachel looked like she was starting to come unraveled, her hair once again trying to escape the confines of its braid, and I had to admit that I was a poor choice to play the Rock of Gibraltar.

Rachel and I went back to turn out her dogs. "I guess I'll have to feed them later," she said as we entered the kennel. "After the police take . . . after the kitchen is cleaned up."

I nodded. "Great. I don't think the police would approve of us 'destroying evidence,' or whatever."

Actually, I had no intention of sharing the kitchen with a corpse, and from the look on Rachel's face, I was certain she felt the same way. It was bad enough that we knew he was there. And, to make matters worse, the pool of blood had started to smell—a sickly-sweet kind of odor.

I was in the process of leading two dogs outside, when one of them broke free and headed toward the far edge of the building. I put his companion in a pen and went after him. He was pawing the ground and pushing his muzzle against the fence. Suddenly his head and shoulders popped through. I grabbed his hind legs to keep him from escaping and called to Rachel.

She came over and fingered the edge of the fence. "This was supposed to have been fixed," she said angrily. "A month ago. The bolts rusted through. I'd forgotten all about it."

"Of course this doesn't explain the kennel door being open," I said.

"No, I don't suppose so."

The grapevine at the dog track works as well as any other, and soon we had a crowd of owners and trainers gawking at us through the chain-link. The crowd grew when a Brightwater Beach patrol car and a Fire Rescue unit stormed onto the premises, their lights flashing and their sirens blaring. All of this I found somewhat unnecessary, since the victim was obviously past resuscitation, and the four-legged perpetrator was halfway to Jacksonville, if she knew what was good for her.

The paramedics approached us and asked to see the body. Rachel pointed toward the kennel door, mumbling "freezer" and something else I didn't catch, and the paramedics went inside with their tackle boxes.

The police officer slowly climbed out of his car and stood up, carefully adjusting his hat and his trousers. He wore dark glasses, which hid his eyes. The rest of his face was devoid of expression. I'd decided long ago that policemen learn in policeman school how to keep their faces blank, no matter what. That way, the bad guys can't tell what they're thinking or how much they know. Detective Weller was pretty good at it, but this guy must have graduated at the top of his class, because he didn't even look in our direction or otherwise acknowledge our existence as he came through the outer door, which was now propped open with a shovel.

He met the paramedics coming out of the kennel. They both looked a little pale, and one of them was gagging, which caused the policeman to hesitate for a second before stepping inside. It wasn't long before he, too, was back outside, but he'd obviously seen worse. He had taken off his glasses, but his face was still blank, and he still didn't look at us as he walked back to his car and began talking on his radio.

"Why isn't he questioning us?" Rachel asked, her voice held to a whisper.

"I don't know. Maybe he's waiting for reinforcements."

The paramedics had recovered, and now they were talking to the cop, who was filling out a form. Rachel and I went back into the kennel to bring out a few more dogs, and almost immediately the policeman appeared in the doorway. I was impressed. He was a lot faster than I figured him to be.

"I'm sorry, ladies," he said, "but you'll have to stay outside, until the crime-scene unit is finished."

Rachel bristled visibly. "We have to let the dogs out to relieve themselves," she said. "Trust me—we won't go near the body."

The cop shook his head. "Can't do that, ma'am. You'll have to stay outside."

In policeman school, I thought, they must teach you to go strictly by the book, no matter what. That way, you don't have to make any decisions or do any creative thinking. "I'll bet if *he* had to go to the bathroom, the rules would be different," I said, not very softly.

Rachel frowned. "I *have* to let those dogs out, somehow," she said.

"Wait until Dr. Augustin gets here," I told her. "You know how persuasive he can be when he decides to go against the system."

She didn't comment, but I could tell she agreed with me, because she smiled faintly.

About fifteen minutes later two unmarked police cars and a large blue-and-white van marked CRIME SCENE INVESTIGATION pulled up next to the patrol car. Five men, three of them in suits and two in coveralls, got out and, after talking briefly to the patrolman and the paramedics, came through the outer door. One of the suits seemed to be in charge, and he came over to Rachel and me.

"Good morning," he said. "I'm Detective Robinson." He showed us his shield and handed Rachel one of his business cards. I peered over her shoulder. It read, *Det. Sgt. Peter Robinson, Homicide Division.* "I guess you two ladies have had quite a morning."

Rachel nodded. Then, to my utter amazement, the detective smiled. Maybe when you get to be a sergeant, I thought, you also get to use your facial muscles.

"I'm concerned about my dogs, Detective," Rachel said. "They need to be let out. They are trained not to soil their crates, and if I don't let them out, it could be very upsetting to them, as well as to me."

"And very messy, too," I added.

The detective appeared to be considering this problem while another man began stringing up yellow plastic tape with the words POLICE LINE—DO NOT CROSS printed every six inches on it. When he had finished, it extended across the outer doorway, along the inner walls and all along the turnout pens, making it nearly impossible to move dogs back and forth. Or people, for that matter. I was surprised no one had asked us to step out into the parking lot, since we were now imprisoned behind "The Line."

"It may be a while longer, I'm afraid," Detective Robinson told us. "But we'll be out of here just as soon as possible. In the meantime I'd like to ask you ladies a few questions." He pointed outside. "Let's get away from all this confusion, shall we?"

I knew it. We ducked under the tape and joined the twenty or so people standing in the parking lot.

He questioned Rachel first, asking me to wait over by the patrolman's car. The patrolman had put his sunglasses back on, and his face was as unreadable as ever. I smiled at him, but it was a waste of time.

When the detective had finished with Rachel, she went over to one of the men leaning against the building, and he put his arm around her. Then the detective motioned for me to join him, which I did.

"Would you like to sit down?" the detective asked, indicating the front seat of his car.

"No, that's all right," I said. "I'll stand, if you don't mind."

He flipped to a clean page in his notebook. "Please tell me your name and where you live," he said, pen poised for action.

"Samantha Holt," I responded, "624 Sabal Palm Court, Apartment Two-B."

Out of the corner of my eye, I saw Dr. Augustin drive up in his Jeep Cherokee. He got out, spoke to Rachel, then marched purposefully over to the yellow tape. Without a second thought, he went under it and disappeared around the corner. From the way he was holding his shoulders, I knew he was preparing for war.

The detective had not seen him and continued with his questions. "And where do you work, Ms. Holt?"

"Paradise Cay Animal Hospital," I told him, and gave him the address.

"What is your relationship to Mrs. Augustin?" he asked.

I had to think for a second who he was talking about. Somehow "Rachel" and "Mrs. Augustin" seemed unlikely synonyms. "I work for Dr. Augustin, Rachel's veterinarian," I said finally.

The detective was taking all of this down in his notebook. "I understand that Mrs. Augustin spent last night at your apartment. Is that correct?"

"Yes," I answered.

"Why was that?" Detective Robinson was looking at me now, smiling.

"Dr. Augustin asked me to, because her house was broken into Friday night, and he was concerned about her." And she wouldn't stay with *him,* though I'm sure he offered, I nearly added.

"Is that why you came along with her this morning?"

"Yes," I answered. There was no point in trying to think of some other reason.

"What time did you and Mrs. Augustin arrive?"

"About eight, I think."

"And when you entered the premises, did you notice anything out of the ordinary or unusual?" he asked.

"I've never been here before," I said, "so I really wouldn't know what was and what wasn't usual for this place. Except the body, of course. Hopefully, that isn't the norm around here."

The corners of his mouth turned up ever so slightly. "You found the body?"

"Yes. I was looking for one of Rachel's dogs who'd gotten out of its cage."

He wrote this down. "Were you acquainted with the decedent?" he asked, now looking at me intently.

Suddenly I was angry. Why did everybody always pussyfoot around the truth when people died? What was wrong with the word *dead,* anyway? I wanted to laugh. Somehow *Night of the Living Decedents* just didn't have the same impact.

"No," I told him. "Rachel said he was a handler here at the track."

I saw Dr. Augustin come back under the yellow tape. He went over to Rachel, who then headed for the kennel. I thought, In policeman school they should warn you about people like Dr. Augustin. It only went to show that the pen, or in this case Dr. Augustin's tongue, *is* mightier than the sword.

"Did you find the dog—the one that was loose?" The detective had turned his head to see what I was looking at, but now was looking back at me.

"Not yet," I answered.

The detective closed his little notebook. "Well, I guess that's all for now, Ms. Holt. As I told Mrs. Augustin, we'll need both of you to come downtown later today to give us a statement. It shouldn't take too long. You'll just be asked to tell what happened and what you saw—that sort of thing. We'll get it down on tape, for the record. Then you can go. Okay?"

He put the notebook in his jacket pocket and the pen in his shirt pocket, and a long-forgotten image of my father flashed through my head, and I wondered if the detective's wife ever got mad because his pen had leaked and ruined his best shirt.

I shook the image aside. "Okay," I said, and turned to go.

The crowd of gawkers had thinned out a bit, but a few were still hanging around like jackals, waiting to gobble up the remaining shreds of gossip.

"Sorry about the inconvenience," I heard the detective say.

I looked back at him and thought how pleasant he had been about everything and how concerned he had seemed to be about us and the dogs. I nodded and walked over to Dr. Augustin.

He looked like the proverbial canary-eating cat. He beamed, the smugness making his face seem broader. Or maybe it was his grin. I almost expected him to disappear, leaving the grin behind.

"I see you convinced them to let Rachel back into the kennel," I said.

"Yes. I said, 'It would be terrible, don't you think, if those poor dogs had to suffer even a few extra minutes because of some stupid, bureaucratic nonsense?' "

"You mean, you pointed out the potential for a lot of very adverse publicity?"

Dr. Augustin grinned, and I saw his smoldering, coal-black eyes flare up briefly. His righteousness will be feasting for some time on this mess, I told myself. I only hope Rachel and the rest of us aren't consumed in the process.

CHAPTER 13

•

The paramedics and the patrolman with facial paralysis left soon after the detective arrived. Then one of the unmarked cars drove off in a cloud of dust. I found out later from Dr. Augustin, it belonged to the division commander. From the way he was driving, I presumed he and Dr. Augustin hadn't exactly hit it off.

The men in coveralls made a couple of trips from the kennel to their van for various items, and soon the detective joined them, leaving Dr. Augustin and me and five gawkers to hold up the wall. I was so tired I could hardly stand.

"Want a Coke?" Dr. Augustin asked me. "Rachel could probably use something right about now." We could hear her dogs barking.

"Sure," I said. "Anything with caffeine in it."

He left.

I slid down the wall to a sitting position and was just closing my eyes, when another unmarked car rolled up. A stoop-shouldered man with graying hair, dressed in an ill-fitting suit that looked like it had been slept in, got out and went around to the trunk. He took out a surprisingly new, modern-looking case, along with a smaller black medical bag, and slammed the trunk closed. Brightwater Beach's version of Quincy, I decided.

He looked a little lost, so I pointed toward the kennel. He nodded and went in. I noticed that his skin had a strange translucent, waxen appearance. Perhaps being around corpses all the time—people who'd died violent, awful deaths—had transformed him. Maybe there was some truth to the old beliefs about vapors and invisible gases emanating from the dead. I glanced down at my hands to see if the short time I was in the company of the "decedent" had had any ill effects on me. They looked pink and healthy, but they were trembling.

Realizing suddenly that I was actually living all of this movie madness made me feel a little sick. I took a few deep breaths and tried to think of something pleasant. Then I heard a lot of growling and snarling and Rachel shouting. The detective appeared at the outer door looking irritated. He called to me and pointed over his shoulder. I got up and raced through the doorway like a runner crossing the finish line, forgetting about the yellow tape, until it was hanging around my middle in a victory embrace. The detective told me never mind.

Rachel was trying to pull two of her dogs apart. One of them had a bloody shoulder, and neither of them was muzzled. Three dogs, also muzzleless, pranced around in the adjoining pen like spectators at a cockfight. The entire police ensemble stood in the kennel doorway watching. I dashed in and grabbed the injured dog by his collar, while Rachel pulled the aggressor out of the pen. I led the wounded animal out and shut the gate.

"Thanks, Sam," she said. She threw a look of disgust in the direction of the five men.

"Why aren't these dogs muzzled?" I asked as I inspected the animal's wound. It was superficial, but would have to be stitched up in order to heal properly.

"Trying to save time, I guess. It was stupid, especially

with these two." Rachel dragged the still-snarling greyhound into the kennel and put him in his cage. I noticed that the men in coveralls gave the dog a wide berth, regarding him like they might an ax murderer.

I led the wounded animal into the kennel after Rachel. "Dr. Augustin will have to put a couple of sutures in this shoulder," I said. "He went to find us something to drink, but is probably back by now. I'll go get him." I looked up at the detective. "If that's okay," I added.

"It would be better if he could work on the dog outside," he said. "To minimize the number of people in here. The less interference we have, the faster we can get out of your hair." He was smiling blandly, and I thought, what a great political future this guy has.

"Sure," I said, "I guess he can."

Rachel took a leash from the wall and hooked the dog, Domino Joe, to his cage. "If you'll just let Samantha and me finish putting my dogs in their cages, we'll be finished and out of here."

The detective quickly agreed.

I'd been watching the medical examiner, craning my neck over the freezer, and I noticed he was sticking something in the corpse's eye.

The detective saw me and said, simply, "Time of death."

"Oh," I said, thinking how I should mention this to P.J. the next time she complained about examining stool samples for worm eggs.

Dr. Augustin was waiting by his Jeep with our drinks, and shook his head when Rachel walked up with Domino. "Why didn't you have the dogs muzzled?" he asked her.

"The cops were pressuring her to finish up, so she was trying to save time," I offered.

Rachel shot me a look that told me thanks, but she didn't need my help, so I shut up. She suddenly looked a lot more in control. "You might as well take him to the clinic and leave him for the night," she told Dr. Augustin. "I simply will not go back in there, until *those people* are gone."

"All right," he said, lifting Domino into the back of his Jeep. He closed the hatchback and turned to me. "You stay with Rachel. I can manage." He picked up his Coke from the vehicle's roof and climbed into the front seat. "We'll need to look for Blue as soon as possible, preferably before dark. I imagine the cops will have Animal Control out looking before too long. It would be better if one of us found her first."

"You'll have to euthanize her, won't you?" I asked, not looking at Rachel.

"I don't see why," he said.

"She killed that Harvey guy, didn't she?"

"Somebody went to a lot of trouble to make it *look* like she did, but I'm not convinced. How many people do you know would stand by quietly and let a dog go for their jugular?"

I shook my head. "No one, I suppose, but why . . . ?"

"Because that guy's arms and hands were clean—not a scratch or bite anywhere." He put his key in the ignition. "I don't know about you, but I'd sure make some effort at defending myself."

"Maybe he was unconscious," Rachel said.

Dr. Augustin nodded. "Precisely. And I doubt even a vicious dog would rip the throat out of somebody lying unconscious on the ground. Chew him up a little, maybe, but nothing more." He paused. "I could be wrong, of course," he said, and I almost laughed, "but I think somebody killed this Harvey character because, after Friday night, he had become a liability. And I think we can all agree on who had the best motive."

He waited for Rachel to say something, drumming his fingers slowly and precisely on the window frame. She looked over at me. I drew my lips together in a grimace and nodded. If Rachel was right about the threats, there could be only one person who would want Harvey Snead dead and, having caused it in the first place, would know enough about Rachel's string of bad luck to take advantage of it.

"Brad Donovan," she said.

Dr. Augustin started the engine. "More than likely," he said. Then he threw the Jeep into gear and departed, leaving Rachel and me to carry on bravely in his absence. And wasn't that just typical, I thought grimly.

CHAPTER 14

•

The rest of that day produced few surprises. After the police finished gathering clues and the body was removed, Rachel and I went into the kennel.

The place was a wreck. There were dirty smudges and dusting powder all over the freezer top and counters. Practically every other surface had evidence of the stuff as well. There was still blood on the floor and on the refrigerator. Add to that bits and pieces of yellow tape, paper, and cellophane, and I felt like a New York sanitation worker after New Year's Eve. Neatness obviously wasn't a police-department requirement.

Rachel mixed up a batch of kennel disinfectant and poured it everywhere, nearly asphyxiating us. Then she pulled the hose in from outside and showered off every trace of what had transpired there, as though she'd been raped and was trying to cleanse her body of the evil. I stood by and watched, not wanting to interfere.

That finished, she pulled several enormous packages of frozen chopped meat marked NOT FOR HUMAN CONSUMPTION from the freezer. She unwrapped them, sawed them in pieces with a well-worn butcher knife, then put them in the sink to thaw. I couldn't help comparing those dark red chunks with the gore we had just witnessed and decided that a diet of tofu and bean sprouts might not be such a bad idea.

At 1:10, Rachel locked the kennel door, pulling on it a couple of times just to make sure. Then we walked out to her car.

"Do you want to pick up something for lunch, before we go to the police station?" she asked. "I'm not really hungry, but I'm starting to get a headache."

Food did not appeal to me right then, either, but I knew we'd both probably feel better if we ate. "Sure," I said. "Is it too early for a beer?"

Rachel looked at her watch. "No. It's past one. Why don't we go up to the Finish Line Lounge? They've got sandwiches and hamburgers there, and the view is nice. We could use a change of scenery, don't you think?"

I agreed.

Rachel drove around to the front. The lot was more than half-full by then, since the matinee started at one. A guard let us park close to the building in one of the spaces marked RESERVED. We walked up two flights of stairs to the bar. That, too, was nearly full. A small table in the corner had just been vacated, and we grabbed it.

I expected to see a lot of shabbily dressed old men drinking cheap whiskey and gambling away their welfare checks. But the crowd was an even mix of young and old. Several women about my age sat at a large round table studying the race program. They were sharing a pitcher of sangria and a large order of nachos.

"I take it none of your dogs is racing today," I said.

"No. I scratched all my entries for this weekend after R.C. died. . . ." She looked away.

"I'm going to the ladies' room," I told her. "Order me a draft, if you would. Anything is fine."

"Okay," Rachel said.

On the way to the rest rooms, I paused to admire the view below us. Eight young men dressed in black pants and white shirts each led a greyhound slowly up the track, single file. As they passed in front of the grandstand each pair stopped for a few seconds. The man adjusted his dog's brightly colored race blanket and pulled up on the lead so the animal posed alertly for the spectators and the camera mounted on the fence. Then they proceeded toward the starting boxes.

In the bright sun, the sandy track appeared almost white, the men and dogs a colorful, carefully orchestrated parade. The shrubbery in the infield had been trimmed to spell out SUMMERLAND, something I'd missed from ground level. The whole effect was rather nice, certainly not seedy, like I'd been led to believe by Mr. Ames. And then I remembered Harvey Snead.

When I returned from the rest rooms, the man I'd seen putting his arm around Rachel that morning was sitting in my chair. He got up.

"This is Paul Connelly," Rachel said. "A fellow kennel owner. Paul, this is Samantha Holt."

We shook hands. He was about five-nine, slender but fit, with short, light brown hair and green eyes. He wasn't exactly handsome, but he had a kind face. I liked him immediately.

"Please join us," I said, sitting down.

He pulled up a chair. "Thank you for helping Rachel out this morning," he said. "I'm sorry you ladies had to go through that. I can't believe one of Rachel's dogs would attack a person, let alone kill one."

Rachel looked angry. "Can we change the subject?"

Paul touched her hand briefly. "I'm sorry, Rachel. That was really stupid." He turned to the bar and signaled the waitress. "They're slow here on Sundays. It's one of their busiest times, but they always seem to be shorthanded."

"I didn't realize so many young people came to the track," I said. "I even saw some families with children on the way in."

Paul laughed. "If you could spend the afternoon outdoors with your family or date and get live entertainment to boot for only a buck, wouldn't you do it? Not everyone comes here to gamble. At least not seriously."

"But where does the money you guys win come from? Don't you need people to bet on the dogs?"

"Not to worry," he said. "There are plenty of hard-core gamblers here every day, believe me." He pointed to three men sitting at the bar, their eyes glued to one of the little closed-circuit TV monitors located at various points around the room. The live view was of the starting boxes. "Take those guys, for instance. I see them in here or downstairs fairly regularly. Real dedicated."

Rachel leaned forward and lowered her voice. "The fat one with the cigar and the man to his right work for the city. The skinny one is a building inspector, I think. Their names escape me. I've never seen the guy on the end before."

"He's a lawyer. Real-estate law, I'm told," Paul said.

The cocktail waitress brought our beers. We decided against hamburgers because of the time, but we wanted something, so Paul ordered us nachos. He lit a cigarette, then inhaled deeply. He hadn't asked if Rachel or I minded, but he thoughtfully blew the smoke up toward the ceiling. I watched it merge with the cloud already floating there like a London fog. David had smoked, I thought idly.

"How long have you raced greyhounds?" I asked Paul.

"About fifteen years," he said. "My uncle owned a kennel out in Kansas. That's where I'm from, originally." He drained his glass, then looked at the clock over the bar. "Well, I'd better be going. I told my trainer I'd be down to help him with the dogs." He turned to Rachel. "Try not to worry. I'll call you later."

The way they looked at each other made me believe there was more to their relationship than just greyhounds.

At three o'clock, Rachel and I drove downtown and gave our statements to Detective Robinson. Everyone at the police station was courteous and efficient, but we had to let them take our fingerprints.

"It's so we can separate out your fingerprints from those of possible suspects," said Detective Robinson. "We do it all the time. Think nothing of it."

But I felt like a criminal, anyway.

I called Dr. Augustin at a few minutes past four. He told us to meet him at the track.

"Blue Moon could be anywhere by now, but it's as good a place as any to start," he said.

Five of us made a thorough search of the area. I called Russell, and he and Paul Connelly arrived in Russell's pickup. Dr. Augustin suddenly grew very cold and business-like when he saw Rachel and Paul together, and I could have counted on one hand the number of times he opened his mouth after that.

We checked out a large parcel of vacant land owned by the county, most of which we had to explore on foot. Even Dr. Augustin's Jeep couldn't get through the palmettos and scrub oak. I kept expecting to be bitten by a rattlesnake and said so to Dr. Augustin. He looked at me like I was a sissy and plowed on ahead, mumbling something about the cold and watch where you put your feet. Three vultures circled overhead.

By 5:30 I had found two shopping carts, a Ninja Turtles

lunch box, a bicycle tire pump, an empty wallet, and eleven old shoes, none of them matching. There was no trace of Blue. Dr. Augustin suggested we call it a day, since the sun was beginning to go down, and with it, the temperature. Nobody protested.

"I'll turn the dogs out and feed them, Rachel," Russell said as we were getting into our cars. "Then I'll make another pass around the track. In case Blue gets hungry and decides to come home."

Rachel shook her head. "You'll do no such thing. This is supposed to be your day off. I can manage." She looked over at me, but before I could say anything, Paul intervened.

"I told Russell I'd be glad to help. Now, you go on back to Samantha's and get a good night's sleep. You look like you're about to pack it in."

I was afraid Rachel might turn down his offer, but she surprised me. "Thanks, Paul. And Russell. Thanks for everything." She smiled at Dr. Augustin, who was leaning against his Jeep, apparently deep in thought.

He stared at her, then nodded. "I'll call you in the morning," he said.

"I really appreciate everything you've done, Samantha," Rachel told me as we entered my apartment. "Letting me stay here, helping me with the dogs . . . you know."

I smiled. "I'm not going to tell you it's been a pleasure, at least not the part this morning. But I've enjoyed having you here. I hope you know you're welcome anytime." I went into the kitchen and opened the refrigerator. "How about Chinese for dinner?" I asked, closing it again.

"No, thank you, I need to get back to my house. Now that Harvey is . . . out of the way . . . I don't think I'm in any danger. I don't think I ever was, really, but you know how Lou is." She didn't sound altogether convinced.

"Really, are you certain you'll be all right?" I asked. "I mean, whoever wants you to keep your mouth shut obviously won't stop at murder. What's to keep him from killing again?"

Rachel paled visibly, and I wanted to kick myself. She obviously did not like imposing on people or admitting that she was afraid. Now she would go home and lie awake with a baseball bat next to her bed.

"It's just that maybe a few more days in the company of others might be a wiser approach," I said quickly. "The police are sure to arrest Donovan or whoever is responsible before too long. Why not stay here till then?" I laughed. "Maybe I'd get to work on time if you were around to wake me up. My cats do their best, but it's a tough job."

Rachel shook her head. Her stubbornness reminded me of her ex-husband. "No, I can't, really. I'm not into living out of a suitcase, and it's hard for me to stick to a schedule when I'm not in my own house. Besides, I don't like leaving my animals alone for more than a day or two."

I could tell she was becoming angry, so I gave it up. She gathered together her things. I watched her neatly fold each piece of clothing, even the dirty ones, and knew she was telling the truth. She was like a cat—meticulous, cautious, determined to make her own choices, uncomfortable in someone else's territory.

"Okay," I said, "but please give me a call, if you need anything."

"Thank you, but I'll be fine. Honest."

I've never actually believed in clairvoyance or sixth senses, but right then I got the strangest feeling that *fine* was definitely not what Rachel was about to be.

CHAPTER 15

•

Monday, February 21

It was cold and dreary. I thought about calling in sick, but figured no one would believe me. I hadn't slept well. I kept seeing Jason in his hockey mask lurking around the corner, butcher knife poised overhead dripping blood. Harvey Snead's blood.

I got to the clinic thirty minutes early. When I opened the front door, I saw Charlie, our resident blood-donor cat, disappear around the corner.

Charlie came to the clinic as a kitten and stayed on, when his owner couldn't pay the bill. Now, in exchange for periodic bloodletting, Charlie is fed and housed and generally doted on by everyone. We let him wander about the clinic during the day, but he is supposed to be in his cage after hours.

"Charlie, you rascal," I called, turning on the light. Dead silence. That was twice in one week that Charlie had spent the night out of his cage. Frank claimed Charlie had learned how to unlatch his door. I found this difficult to believe, since nobody had ever witnessed it.

I made coffee and turned on the various instruments that needed to warm up. I checked the appointment book, hoping all the while that P.J. was well enough to come back to work. Out first appointment was Mrs. Winter. Cynthia had written *Check skin* under *Complaint,* but I doubted there was anything wrong with Frosty's skin. My guess was Mrs. Winter needed her biweekly fix of Augustin charm. I sighed and went to look for the alleged Houdini.

Cynthia met me as I was coming out of the bathroom. "Samantha, somebody left the door to that German shepherd's cage open last night. The one in Isolation. No harm done, fortunately, although I doubt 'you know who' would be too happy if he knew an animal was wandering loose around the clinic at night." She pulled her lips together disapprovingly. "Frank certainly is getting sloppy all of a sudden."

"Looks like it. You might want to check your supply of paper clips and rubber bands. He left Charlie out, too, apparently."

We went into the lab, and I poured us each a cup of coffee. Dr. Augustin hadn't shown up yet, and it was nice to have a few minutes alone to talk with Cynthia.

"I think it's just *terrible* about what happened yesterday," she said. "Is it true that you and Rachel found the . . . body?"

"Yes. And it was pretty nasty." I shuddered and tried to block out the image.

"What happened? This morning's paper said the police think he was killed by one of Rachel's dogs during a robbery attempt. Is that true?"

I shrugged. "It certainly looked that way to me. Dr. Augustin, however, thinks it was murder."

Cynthia gasped. She put her cup on the counter and lowered her voice. "Murder?" she whispered, as if the clinic had a bug in every room. "But who . . . oh, my . . . surely not . . . ?"

"Rachel? No, I don't think so. Dr. Augustin believes it's whoever has been responsible for drugging her dogs. The dead guy was the one she saw leaving her property Friday night. That's why the police think it was a robbery attempt. Rachel still refuses to tell them about the phone calls."

"Why not?"

"I suppose it's because she doesn't think they'll believe her. She doesn't have any proof, after all."

"Dear me," Cynthia said.

At nine o'clock, Dr. Augustin barreled into the surgery, his face threatening, like the sky outside.

"Have you seen this morning's paper?" he snarled.

"Yes," I said. "I noticed they spelled my name correctly." I turned quickly around and began unloading the autoclave.

"I don't mean the article about Snead. I mean this asinine letter to the editor."

I heard the rustle of newsprint, then Dr. Augustin thrust the front section, roughly folded to the editorial page, under my nose. I took it from him and quickly scanned the letter.

"*This* one," he snapped, pointing to the upper left corner with an authoritative index finger.

> EDITOR: The recent rash of maulings by dogs from the Suncoast Kennel Club is only one example of an insidious threat to our community. The Summerland Greyhound Track is a known hangout for drug pushers and prostitutes, and is within shouting distance of a day-care center and three residential subdivisions. How can we, the taxpayers of Brightwater Beach, expect to raise our children in a safe, crime-free environment, when there is evil lurking in our own backyards?

It was signed, *J. W. Ames.*

Dr. Augustin snatched the paper from me and flung it into the trash can. "This thing with Harvey Snead will only serve to draw attention to Ames and his moronic cause." He paced around the surgery, straightening things on the counters, checking for dust.

I knew he was looking for something to complain about. "Yes, I suppose so," I said. I didn't know what he expected *me* to do about it. I wanted to drop the whole matter. In less then twenty minutes Mrs. Winter would arrive with Frosty, and we still had two cats to neuter. I cleared my throat.

Dr. Augustin stopped pacing and looked at his watch.

"My God, Samantha, do you see what time it is? Why didn't you *say* something?"

Frank finally located Charlie just before noon, asleep on a forty-pound bag of dog food high up in the supply closet behind Cynthia's desk. I questioned him about leaving the cat out Sunday night, but he swore everyone was locked up tight, including the shepherd. I had my doubts, but I was not about to say anything to Dr. Augustin. No one deserved that.

By 1:45, we had finished with our morning clients, and Dr. Augustin left for his usual meal of red meat and grease up the street. I had fended off questions about my Sunday outing six times by then. I was considering taping some appropriate response so I could play it back for the afternoon appointments. Dr. Augustin was obviously tired of the notoriety his clinic was acquiring. The number of Monday walk-ins was up, and we still had the afternoon's crowd to see. I suspected he was also sick of all the attention I was getting, although I couldn't be absolutely sure.

Cynthia didn't bother to go home for lunch. Instead she

and I shared my salad and yogurt and carefully avoided discussing Rachel or Harvey Snead.

I told Cynthia about my date with Michael. We both agreed I would probably have to dodge his wife's ghost from time to time, if I wanted to continue seeing him, which wasn't a sure thing by any means.

"I didn't think his age would make a difference, but he's so conservative," I told her.

Cynthia laughed. "Honey, there are plenty of perfectly normal thirty-year-olds out there who would give anything to be just like Michael Halsey, conservative clothes, BMW, and all. No . . . what's making you nervous is the forty-foot boat and the dinner at Tuttles, though, for the life of me, I can't imagine why."

I walked over to the plate glass and stared out at the darkening sky. "It's not the money," I said quietly. "It's what the money does to people." I turned around and looked at Cynthia. She was smiling sympathetically. "I thought I left all that back home with Lola Longlegs and the candy-apple-red Ferrari."

Cynthia had been idly flipping through the newspaper as we talked. Suddenly she stopped. "Look at this, Samantha. Our own Mrs. Winter."

I went behind the reception desk and peered over her shoulder. She had her finger on a photograph showing a group of middle-aged women dressed in formal attire. I recognized Mrs. Winter and Sylvia Rheems immediately. All of the women were smiling cordially but looked bored, as if being in the paper was an everyday occurrence. I knew from my father's circle of friends that it was an expression that took years of training to perfect.

Mrs. Winter was wearing a black or very dark blue floor-length gown covered with sequins that clung to her body like shrink wrap. I couldn't tell what Sylvia had on. She was standing in the back row. The caption read, *Members of the Beach Key Club dance the night away at the club's annual charity ball, held recently at the home of Mrs. Glynnis Winter, widow of the late Circuit Judge Jameson Winter.* Then it gave the women's names. An accompanying article told about the club's latest endeavor—a neonatal unit at St. Luke's Hospital.

Cynthia looked up at me. "I didn't realize Mrs. Winter and Mrs. Rheems knew each other. Did you?"

"No. But that probably explains how Sylvia found out about Dr. Augustin. It's sort of like sharing the name of your hairdresser or the pool man."

Before Cynthia could respond, the telephone rang. After picking it up, she pressed the "Hold" button. "It's your rich, conservative, almost fifty-year-old admirer," she announced, grinning.

I pointed toward the hall extension and headed that way. "Hello," I answered after a moment, in what I hoped was a very businesslike tone.

"Samantha! What a pleasure to hear your voice. You have no idea what my day has been like so far. Listen, how about a drink after work? I want you to tell me all about your adventure yesterday. Now . . . I won't take no for an answer. When do you get off tonight?"

His thyroid was working overtime again, and I knew it was pointless to resist. "Hopefully, around six," I said.

"Great! I'll pick you up at the clinic, okay?"

"Sure. I guess so."

"Super! See you then." He hung up.

I was still holding the receiver when Cynthia stuck her head around the corner to tell me our next client had arrived. The grin on her face had broadened.

• • •

Michael arrived promptly at six o'clock. Cynthia was fighting with the computer, as usual. Over the intercom she said, "Your ride is here." Dr. Augustin was out of earshot, but it was nice of her to avoid Michael's name.

When I finally finished up with the evening's treatments, I washed my face and hands and combed my hair, then went out to the reception room. I found Michael and Cynthia sitting at her desk, staring at the computer terminal. I noticed that the jar containing the dog heart had disappeared, and in its place sat Charlie like an ebony statue, his green eyes intent on the flickering images playing across the screen.

Michael was explaining something to Cynthia. His hands and mouth moved in unison. The thought of an evening listening to his high-speed conversation, with or without the benefit of alcohol, made me feel more tired than I already was. I smiled and tried to look lively.

"Hi," I said as I entered the room.

They both glanced up.

"Oh, Sam," Cynthia exclaimed. "Mike is a real computer whiz." So now it was "Mike," was it? "He's shown me a shortcut to closing out. I've asked him if he needs a job."

She looked like she had gone into some kind of rapture, and I feared she had succumbed to his warm hands and his eau de pine cologne. I decided it was pretty sneaky of him to get at me through Cynthia, and resolved not to let her enthusiasm cloud my judgment.

"Dr. Augustin will be pleased to hear you've cut Cynthia's overtime in half," I told him. "Now . . . if you can just figure out how to reduce mine."

He stood up and held out his hands, palms facing forward. "No way," he said, laughing. "The thought of all those needles and blood." He made a face and shivered. "No, I think I'll just stick to computers and the newspaper business."

I was about to ask him how he handled reporting about car wrecks and murders if the sight of blood upset him, but he was already saying good-bye to Cynthia, making certain that he shook her hand.

CHAPTER 16

•

It had started to drizzle, a quiet, almost invisible mist that made for dangerous driving and frizzy hair. Michael and I arrived at the Rose and Crown before the usual Monday-night crowd, so there were stools free at the bar. I wanted to avoid sitting at a table, since at the bar it is more difficult to gaze longingly into the eyes of your companion.

The skinny brunette was at her regular roost by the waitress stand. Getting the bartender's attention proved to be somewhat of a challenge for Michael, but he finally succeeded. I knew there would be no tip from us that night.

I asked for my usual. Michael ordered a glass of wine. He wasn't much of a beer drinker, he said. I knew he would rather have had a Scotch and soda at the Holiday Inn, but I wanted home-field advantage for a change.

"So . . . have you recovered from yesterday?" he asked me, after we'd gotten our drinks.

"I guess so," I said. I wanted to tell him that having to constantly sidestep a play-by-play account was actually more stressful than the incident itself. But I didn't, in the hopes he would let it go.

"The dog that did it . . . has anyone found him yet?"

"Her," I said. "Blue Moon. No, not yet. We checked around yesterday afternoon, but there was no sign of her."

"What do you suppose this Harvey Snead was after?"

The way he asked the question made me look to see if he had his little notebook with him. "I have no idea," I said truthfully.

"It was the same guy that Mrs. Augustin saw leaving her property Friday night, wasn't it?"

He was smiling at me, but the face I saw wasn't the face of a lonely widower engaged in romantic prattle. It was the face of a seasoned hunter, alert, taut with anticipation. Hungry. He couldn't help himself. The faint smell of a story was overpowering.

"Yes," I said reluctantly. I wanted to change the subject, but Michael was like a crow, relentlessly pecking away at the eyes of a dead cat. The image frightened me. This whole affair is making me crazy, I thought.

"Have there been many cases of greyhounds attacking and killing people?" he asked.

I felt certain he already knew the answer. He could search through the *Times* computer he was so fond of and come up with far more information than I could ever provide. So why was he pumping me? "I'm not a good person to ask that," I said. "My experience with greyhounds has been limited to Rachel's dogs."

"I see," he said. "Well, can you think of any reason why *her* greyhounds have been attacking people lately?"

He turned his stool around and brought his face quite close to mine. His expression was a carefully arranged mixture of concern and sympathy, with only a trace of interest. Under normal circumstances, I probably would have succumbed and given him the formula for Coca-Cola, if I'd had it. But, at that moment, Rachel and Dr. Augustin came in the back door. They sat down at a corner table.

Suddenly my thoughts turned to escape. "No, I sure

can't," I said, pointedly looking at my watch. "Oh my gosh," I exclaimed. "I was supposed to call my mother at seven-thirty." I smiled innocently, amazed at how easy the lie had been. "Today is her birthday."

So Michael paid for our drinks, and we left, apparently without Dr. Augustin spotting me. I realized, with some amusement that, like the bartender, Michael would be one tip shy that night.

CHAPTER 17

•

Thursday, February 24

I hadn't heard a thing from Michael since Monday. I'm not sure who was more concerned, me or Cynthia. After our abrupt departure from the Rose and Crown, Michael dropped me off at the clinic so I could get my car. He said "Good night," without so much as a peck on the cheek. I was relieved good old Mary hadn't made any unearthly appearances. The fact that Michael asked me out so he could interrogate me didn't help him any, however.

Nothing unpleasant happened to Rachel during the four days following Snead's death. At least, nothing Dr. Augustin cared to discuss.

Dr. Augustin finally stopped foaming at the mouth after Ames's letter failed to gain any public support. I suspected he was working on a rebuttal. I could hear his typewriter clacking away whenever we weren't busy.

Blue Moon was still among the missing. Presumably she was still among the living; however, I feared that might change if she ever turned up.

The weather Thursday was near perfect. It took me five extra minutes to reach the clinic, because the snowbirds were already headed for the beach and their daily dose of the ultraviolet. Dr. Augustin arrived just after I did. He seemed in a pretty good mood and hummed quietly to himself as we went about that morning's surgeries.

We were just finishing up when Cynthia announced over the intercom that I had a visitor. Dr. Augustin motioned for me to go on, that he would watch our patient until I got back.

I trotted happily down the hall, expecting to find Michael standing beside Cynthia's desk. I was disappointed when I saw Mrs. Ames waiting there. She was alone, her children apparently left with a very devoted relative or a masochistic neighbor.

"I told Mrs. Ames that you and Dr. Augustin were in surgery," Cynthia said, obviously irritated at Mrs. Ames, who, like her husband, was not easily put off.

"We are contacting everyone we think might be interested, to let them know about tonight's commission meeting," Mrs. Ames informed me. Again, that unknown entity *we*. I wondered if the Ameses were using it in the royal sense.

"They will be discussing that ridiculous greyhound adoption program the Suncoast Kennel Club has seen fit to institute over at the dog track. *We* are going to convince the commission to abolish it immediately. Certainly you, Miss Holt, should realize how dangerous those dogs are. It's bad enough they live there at the track within striking distance of innocent people, without trying to pass them off as pets to unsuspecting families."

An image of four-headed creatures with fangs instantly came to mind, and I suppressed a smile.

"And anyway," she continued, "it's undoubtedly just an excuse to bring in more kennel owners and more dogs." She arched her brows and shook her head.

I noticed for the first time that Mrs. Ames bit her

fingernails. In fact, she was working on a thumb as she waited for me to respond.

"I appreciate you stopping by, Mrs. Ames," I said, without enthusiasm. "And I'll be sure to tell Dr. Augustin about the meeting, but I believe he was already planning to attend. He usually does, you know." I smiled at her.

She seemed confused, as if she had been prepared to debate the greyhound issue with me or Dr. Augustin, and now was left high and dry like some powerboat at low tide, her prop turning uselessly in the air. "Well, that's fine, then," she said finally. "See you there." She hitched up the shoulder strap of her purse and left.

I watched as she trudged across the parking lot, noticing that the hem of her skirt had come unsewn.

Cynthia shook her head solemnly. "You know Rachel was responsible for starting that program, don't you?" she asked me. "As if she didn't have enough to worry about already."

I nodded. "And it's not just Rachel who has to contend with all this," I said gloomily.

"Good point."

CHAPTER 18

•

We were fifteen minutes late. Dr. Augustin had to park on the street, nearly a block from City Hall.

"Are these meetings usually this crowded?" I asked as we climbed out of his Jeep.

"Depends on the agenda," he said. "I can't believe all these people are interested in what happens at the dog track. Some developer is probably requesting a zoning variance."

The sun was just melting into the sea directly behind us. A pale orange glow illuminated the faces of the people clustered in little groups in front of the building. I recognized several of our clients. Carl Meyerson, Missy's owner, was there, along with his wife. The Ameses were wandering around, undoubtedly marshaling their forces. Mr. Ames was dressed in tan slacks, a pale-colored work shirt, and work boots. In the fading sunlight, he looked like a military officer directing his troops on maneuvers.

"There's Rachel," Dr. Augustin said.

He waved at her, and she met us on the steps. She was wearing a navy-and-white-striped shirtwaist and a navy cable-knit sweater. Because of her height, the skirt nearly touched the ground. Her hair was pulled back in a ponytail and tied with a navy scarf. I barely recognized her.

"Quite a turnout, isn't there?" she asked us. She looked

angry. "Hardly anyone from Suncoast is here. Only the assistant general manager, his consultant, and one other kennel owner. That Ames guy apparently has been on the phone all day calling people, whipping them into a frenzy over this."

"Now, Rachel," Dr. Augustin started, but he didn't get a chance to finish. Mr. Ames's voice boomed out across the parking lot. Heads turned at the sound. He was standing on the hood of a car parked beneath a streetlight. He held a cordless microphone in one hand and a sheet of paper in the other.

"Those of you who have come to help shut down the Summerland Greyhound Track, welcome," he said through the microphone. "We cannot allow the dangers that track and its clientele pose to our families, our children, to continue. We must convince the commission that an expansion of the track is not in the best interests of our community. This is a first step toward closing it down altogether. Those of you who wish to make statements in support of our efforts, please see me now. Thank you."

He hopped off the car. Several people cheered and clapped, and a few flash units went off. It was then that I saw Michael. He and one of the photographers were standing to Mr. Ames's left. Great, I thought. The press is going to make Ames out to be a hero, and Dr. Augustin will be impossible for days.

"Ames is an asshole," Dr. Augustin said suddenly. I glanced over at Rachel. Even in the waning light, I could tell she was nodding in agreement.

"Why is Ames so concerned about public safety?" I asked. "I thought he was against greyhound racing because he feels it's an animal-cruelty issue. You know, 'tiny cages,' 'dogs put to death by the thousands.' "

"I guess he knows he won't get enough people worked up, unless it involves some danger to the community," Dr. Augustin replied. "I never said he was stupid." He took Rachel's arm. "Let's go see if there are any seats left."

The three of us went inside. The room was rapidly filling up. We made our way to the back row and sat down, passing Michael and the photographer on the way. Michael was busy writing and didn't see me.

"I guess it's fortunate we're not closer to the front," Dr. Augustin whispered. "If we stay out of sight and keep our mouths shut, we're less likely to get lynched."

I was surprised at his sudden bout of pacifism, but from the way he was looking at Rachel, I guessed he meant it more for her benefit than for mine. Rachel didn't say anything, but her expression was hardly tranquil.

We sat through two service awards, the reading of the minutes from the previous meeting, and a lively discussion regarding the funding of improvements to the local baseball team's clubhouse, which was located on city property. The team was really only "ours" during spring training. It was, nevertheless, extremely popular with the snowbirds, many of whom hailed from the team's summer home. Providing the players with only the best had long been a pet project of Commissioner Tohlman, obviously an avid sports fan (and beer drinker, if his potbelly was any indication).

The argument centered around the fact that twenty-five thousand dollars seemed, to the mayor at least, to be an awful lot of money, considering the city was supposed to be in the midst of an austerity program. Commissioner Tohlman, an unlit cigar bouncing rhythmically up and down from one corner of his mouth, talked about liabilities such as termites and leaky plumbing, and the fact that a neighboring city had recently begun romancing the team. He finished up with those magic words, *tourist dollars,* and the vote wasn't even close.

Finally the mayor called on the city manager to bring up any items that the staff had voiced concerns over, or that the public had requested the commission take a closer look at. A hush fell over the room.

"Preliminary site plan for a new kennel building and associated visitor parking area for the Suncoast Kennel Club, Incorporated, located approximately one half mile due south of Summerland Boulevard, adjacent to the Summerland Greyhound Track," read the city manager.

The audience began to buzz like a swarm of killer bees.

The mayor, her bobbed hair shining like polished silver beneath the flood of fluorescent lighting, rapped her gavel gently, but firmly, a couple of times. "We'll have order here, or I'll clear the room," she said into her mike. "Is that understood?"

She was staring down at Joseph Ames, who, along with his wife and several apparent supporters, was sitting in the middle of the front row. The buzzing died down. "Have those individuals wishing to speak either for or against the project signed in with the clerk?" the mayor continued. "If not, please do so at this time." She indicated the staff table to her right, where two secretaries were busy recording the proceedings. "Is the person representing the project present?" she asked.

An overweight, balding man in his midfifties rose and shuffled forward. Several people in the vicinity of Mr. Ames booed, but stopped when the mayor picked up her gavel and glared. The man stepped up to the podium, which was located about fifteen feet in front of the rostrum, searched through some papers he had brought with him, then leaned into the microphone. His voice was breathy and pitched a little too high, but, I thought, it goes nicely with his general appearance—soft, nonthreatening, probably henpecked. A poor match for Joseph Ames.

He identified himself as Thomas Rheems, Assistant General Manager for the Suncoast Kennel Club, Inc.

"Somehow I knew Sylvia's husband would be a wimp," Dr. Augustin whispered. "But you've got to feel sorry for anyone married to *that* woman."

Mr. Rheems cleared his throat several times, then briefly outlined the project, while another man, presumably the track's consulting architect, walked from one commissioner to another, displaying a large piece of poster board, which, Mr. Rheems said, gave a layout of the proposed building and parking lot. Then Mr. Rheems held up a sheet of paper and began reading.

"In summary, I would like to say that the Suncoast Kennel Club is proud to offer this new facility free of charge to local breeders and racing kennels. It is our hope that they will become ardent supporters of the retired greyhound adoption program begun last year by Mrs. Rachel Augustin, herself a racing kennel owner. Dogs housed in the facility will be cared for by trained personnel, with the club paying all expenses. We also hope that other greyhound tracks throughout the country will follow our lead and provide an alternative to euthanasia for these magnificent animals. Thank you."

The booing started up again, but Rheems was finished. He gathered together his papers.

The mayor banged her gavel sharply, and the room grew quiet. "Are there any questions from the staff or the commission?" she asked, looking to her right and then to her left.

The rostrum's occupants and those seated at the staff table

eyed each other halfheartedly. After a moment Stanley Tohlman removed his cigar and leaned into his microphone.

"I think Mr. Rheems and the Suncoast Kennel Club are to be commended for this worthwhile project," he said, smiling at Mr. Rheems like they were long-lost buddies. Then he turned his attention to Joseph Ames, and the smile vanished. "I wish to remind those in attendance here tonight that the city receives a large portion of its annual revenue from the operation of the Summerland Greyhound Track. Should we lose that source of income, it would become necessary to make up the difference someplace else." He stuck the cigar back in his mouth, but continued to stare at Mr. Ames. The specter of "taxes" danced silently around the room.

"Mr. Rheems," the mayor began, ignoring Commissioner Tohlman completely, "you understand this discussion is solely for the purpose of providing those interested with information, and that no vote is required or intended at this time?"

Mr. Rheems nodded, then picked up his papers and plodded slowly back to his seat on the fourth row.

"All right then, Mr. Ames," the mayor continued, "I believe you have something to say?"

Joseph Ames stood up and started toward the podium, amid scattered clapping and cheering. The mayor picked up her gavel but put it down again. Once at the microphone, Ames gave his name and address in the clear, authoritative tone I'd grown used to hearing. Then he launched into his well-practiced speech about the perils of the Summerland Greyhound Track, adding colorful references to Harvey Snead and the little girl who'd been attacked by Rachel's dog Magic. He could have been talking to a bunch of mannequins, for all the response he got out of the commission. They'd apparently experienced Mr. Ames before.

Rachel, on the other hand, shifted around in her chair, as if about to hop up and race down the aisle. Dr. Augustin put his hand on her arm. She looked up at him but didn't smile.

The buzzer on the clerk's desk went off, and Mr. Ames hastily finished up, then went back to his chair. The room burst into applause, and the mayor smacked her gavel smartly against the desk, demanding silence.

Next up was, to our utter amazement, Mr. Meyerson. He'd brought slides with him, one of which he handed to the clerk, who slipped it into the projector mounted on the wall to the right of the rostrum.

Mr. Meyerson was considerably less confident in his manner than Mr. Ames had been. In a slightly halting voice, he gave his name and address, then a short recitation about his Yorkie's unfortunate encounter with Rachel's dog—one she had only that morning "farmed out," as he put it. He stressed how the creature was an example of what would be housed at the proposed kennel. Then he asked the clerk to show his slide.

If the commissioners were asleep during Mr. Ames's stint at the podium, they were awake now, with the possible exception of Stanley Tohlman, who looked thoroughly bored. The slide was a picture of Missy right after the Meyersons had taken her home from the clinic. Whoever had done the photography obviously knew his stuff. I could see clearly every one of Dr. Augustin's neat, even sutures, the shaved, swollen body and tiny aluminum brace that surrounded the Yorkie's hind leg, the look of pain and fear in her eyes.

"Meyerson must have taken that picture for insurance purposes," Dr. Augustin said, under his breath. "What *I* don't understand is how he could get himself hooked up with a guy like Ames. I thought he was smarter than that."

"I do not have a picture of Missy before the surgery," Mr. Meyerson was saying into the microphone, "but you can certainly see from this slide that her injuries were extensive."

The sole female commissioner, a petite woman with carrot-red hair and long red fingernails, looked faint, and the mayor asked for the slide projector to be turned off, posthaste.

"Thank you, Mr. Meyerson," the mayor said hurriedly. "Are there any other individuals who wish to speak for or against the project?"

For a second I thought it was over. That Mr. Ames had failed to sway any of the commissioners, despite Harvey Snead and Missy Meyerson and the little girl from the trailer park. Even the woman with red hair looked like she had regained her composure and was ready to move on. Then, before Mr. Augustin could grab her, Rachel sprang from her seat and headed up the aisle. Dr. Augustin frowned, then glanced at me and shrugged.

When Rachel got to the podium, she reached up and yanked the microphone down as far as it would go. She still had to crane her neck to be heard.

"My name is Rachel Augustin," she said clearly and firmly. "I live at 722 Deerfield Lane, Skelton. I would like to say a few words in support of the kennel addition at the Summerland Greyhound Track." She paused, as though waiting for the audience to boo and heckle her, but you could hear a pin drop, the room was so quiet.

"Whether you agree with the idea of greyhound racing or not," she continued, "I'm sure most of you hate the practice of killing healthy dogs, just because they can't win races anymore."

Several people nodded enthusiastically.

"Greyhounds make wonderful pets. Even the ones raised in a kennel environment are sweet-tempered around people. They wear muzzles when they race to keep them from nipping at each other, not to keep them from biting their handlers." Suddenly Mr. Ames jumped up.

"Then how do you explain the attacks by *your* dogs, Mrs. Augustin? Unprovoked attacks that resulted in injury, even death."

The mayor twitched and raised her gavel, then put it down. I guess she figured it was a legitimate question, even *if* Mr. Ames was speaking out of turn.

The TV cameraman was having trouble deciding where to point his camera. He kept swinging it from the podium to the front row and back again. Mr. Ames stood, hands on hips, towering over Rachel, even from ten feet away. Rachel, to her credit, remained in complete control. She didn't scream or cry, or jump up and down, or call Mr. Ames any dirty names. She grabbed hold of the podium with both hands and stretched her neck out like a chicken.

"That's easy, Mr. Ames," she said into the mike. "I have proof that my dogs were under the influence of drugs. Given to them without my knowledge by someone who wants to discredit me. And all because I'm not afraid to speak out against those who give greyhound racing a bad name."

Cameras clicked, tape recorders whirred, and I could see Michael bent over his notepad. The commissioners watched Rachel, most of them without any discernible reaction. Only the mayor looked embarrassed, and Stanley Tohlman's cigar jerked up and down like a piston. For a minute I thought he was going to bite off the end and swallow it. I turned to Dr. Augustin. He was shaking his head, his eyes closed.

"God, Rachel, what have you done?" he murmured quietly.

Rachel stepped down from the podium and walked briskly across the room. Mr. Rheems, his consultant, and Rachel's friend Paul Connelly got up and followed her out the door.

The mayor gave up trying to regain order and called for a ten-minute break. As soon as we could, Dr. Augustin and I made our way through the crowd of people clogging the hallway and exits, eager to leave now that the main event was over. I looked for Michael, but he was gone.

CHAPTER 19

•

Friday, February 25

Cynthia held up the city and state section of the *Times*. The headline read, TROUBLE BREWING AT SUMMERLAND—CITIZEN GROUP PROTESTS GREYHOUND PROGRAM. It had Michael's byline. "The police sure know about Rachel's dogs *now,* don't they?" she asked me.

"I can't say I blame Rachel for losing it," I remarked. "Ames obviously isn't above melodrama in order to recruit supporters."

"I watched the meeting on TV. Your Mr. Halsey wrote a very balanced story, don't you think?" Cynthia was smiling, hopeful, I supposed, that Michael and I would soon become an "item," as my mother liked to call it.

"He's not *my* Mr. Halsey, Cynthia," I growled. The smile faded and she folded up the paper.

"Whatever," she said, not trying to hide the hurt.

I loved Cynthia, but God, she was just like my mother! As if being single was a sin second only to being barren. "Yes," I said softly. "He did a nice job. Even Dr. Augustin had better not complain about it."

The phone rang, and I headed for the kennel to remind Frank that Mad Max was coming in to board for two weeks. The thought of Frank struggling every day to care for a dog that weighed twice what he did perked me up considerably.

Michael dropped by at three, his usually cheerful expression replaced by a more somber one.

"Greetings!" I said from behind the reception desk. The waiting room was empty for a change. Cynthia had gone to the post office, and Dr. Augustin was out on one of his rare house calls.

"Samantha, I'm afraid I'm the bearer of bad tidings." Michael came over to the desk and leaned against it. "The coroner's report just came back," he told me. I was silent. Michael went over to one of the reception chairs and sat down. "It was murder. The dog didn't do it. Someone just made it *look* that way." He grimaced. "Snead's throat was cut with a knife, then ripped apart using some kind of tree-trimmer thing. To make it look like tooth marks, I guess." He rubbed the back of his neck. "Apparently, he was hit over the head first. He was unconscious, but not dead, when his veins were severed."

When I didn't say anything, he glanced up at me. "You don't look surprised," he said accusingly, then came back over to the desk. "Somebody beat me to the punch, or what?"

I studied his face for a moment, trying to see past the warm, handsome exterior. I was not a particularly good judge of character, that I knew, but I wanted desperately to trust him. I was tired of our thrust-and-parry conversations. Besides, he was obviously a good source of information.

"Nobody beat you to the punch, Michael," I said. "Dr. Augustin decided right from the start it was probably murder."

The phone rang, and I answered it. Michael went back to his chair. After I hung up, I continued. "Like she said last night, somebody has been drugging her dogs, trying to make her look bad. She thinks Harvey Snead was working for the guy."

Michael was staring at me, his face stony, unreadable. I felt the need to make excuses, to apologize.

"I didn't tell you Monday, because . . . in the first place, I don't like to be grilled. And in the second place, Dr. Augustin warned us not to talk to the press. Reporters are not among his favorite people, if you want to know the truth." I wasn't doing a very good job. "Of course, he doesn't know *you,* now, does he?"

Michael was still staring at me, but I could see a faint smile beginning to soften his features, the furrows at the corners of his eyes deepening. He wants me to feel guilty, I thought.

"Damn you, Michael!" I shouted. The phone rang again, and I let it go. After several moments someone in back picked it up.

Suddenly Michael laughed. "It's nice to know I have this effect on you, Samantha." He stood up. "So, tell me, what has Mrs. Augustin done to warrant something as serious as murder?" When I didn't answer right away, he held up his hands teasingly. "See, no notebook, no tape recorder. I'm clean. I swear."

So I told him. All of it. Halfway through my story, Cynthia returned, and I had to pause long enough for Michael to give her a brotherly hug and say how nice she looked and squeeze her hand. She blushed like a schoolgirl.

"I'll see what I can find out about this dog-food company," Michael told me when I had finished. "Maybe there's some connection between the company's owners and Bradley Donovan. Maybe he's a shareholder or partner. That might explain why he is so concerned about the rest of the owners and trainers going someplace else for their meat."

He reached across the desk and tore a sheet of paper from Cynthia's notepad, then began writing on it. "Still . . . it would have to involve an awful lot of money to justify murder, I should think."

"Rachel has never gotten along with Brad Donovan," Cynthia interjected. "She found out he was using live rabbits to train his dogs. Jackrabbits imported from Kansas, or someplace. She turned him in."

"Nice guy," Michael said. "Sure sounds like he would have reason to want Rachel out of the racing business, and like money, vengeance makes a great motive for murder."

As he talked I watched Dr. Augustin drive into the parking lot. Michael followed my gaze, then cleared his throat.

"I think this is my cue to shove off," he said. He touched my arm. "I'll call you as soon as I have something, Samantha." He nodded toward Cynthia. "You two take care, now."

We said our good-byes, and he left. Cynthia was smiling at me, but she didn't say anything. The silence was awkward, but brief, since right behind Dr. Augustin came Mr. Clark with Mad Max. I took off for the lab, leaving Cynthia to call Frank on the intercom.

CHAPTER 20

•

Saturday, February 26

Trouble usually comes in threes, according to that old wives' tale. By my count, Harvey Snead's death was number seven, if you started with Missy Meyerson.

When Dr. Augustin failed to show for his nine o'clock Saturday, I started calling around. I finally found him at the police station.

"They're holding Rachel on two counts of first-degree murder," he said.

"What?"

"Bradley Donovan was killed around midnight last night. Stabbed with Rachel's butcher knife and dumped in the bushes out by the kennel parking lot. A guard found him early this morning."

I was numb. "Oh," I said stupidly.

"Rachel checked out of the kennel at eleven last night, right after Russell. She went straight home. No witnesses, of course."

"Have you been able to talk to her?"

"No, not yet. My lawyer, Matthew Kemp, is trying to get her out on bail, but he's not hopeful. They've got her for Snead's death, too."

I heard a lot of noise at his end, and voices telling him to hurry up.

"I've got to go, Sam. Take care of things for me, will you? I'll be in as soon as I can." He hung up.

I called Cynthia back to the lab and told her and P.J. what had happened. Neither of them looked very surprised or distraught. I figured they were numb, too. The nightmare had grown too large. It had taken on a surreal quality. This isn't happening, our brains told us. Ignore it.

"What should we do about the appointments?" Cynthia asked me. "The waiting room is filling up."

I thought for a minute. My first impulse was to close the clinic. Put a sign on the door saying there had been a death in the family. But I knew we would be letting Dr. Augustin down. Admitting defeat. He needed to know we could carry on without him, at least for a little while. But that was only part of it. *I* needed to know we could carry on without him. Besides, it was Saturday. How bad could it get?

"Call Larry at the emergency clinic and see if he would be willing to waive the emergency charges on anything we refer to him. Explain that we'll only send over the most serious cases—things that won't wait."

She agreed and went out front.

By midafternoon, my head was throbbing so violently I feared I was on the verge of a stroke. I had to squint to keep my eyeballs from popping out of their sockets. Of course, we'd only referred one patient to Dr. Wilson, but that was small comfort. It had been necessary to tell four clients they would have to make another appointment to see Dr. Augustin. A "follow-up visit" I had called it, but the really savvy ones knew it was because I was afraid to prescribe medication without Dr. Augustin's approval. They didn't say anything, but I could see it in their eyes.

At two, Mrs. Thomas Rheems, dressed like she had just

come from having tea with the queen, arrived with Pepe. She actually had an appointment. Oddly, she didn't seem upset about Dr. Augustin's absence and even smiled when I came in the room. I wasn't sure why she was there. Her dog's ear looked fine to me, but she insisted it still bothered him.

While I examined Pepe Mrs. Rheems babbled on about nothing in particular, complaining about the weather, the tourists, her housekeeper. Suddenly I realized she was talking about Rachel.

"It's just terrible about Mrs. Augustin," she said. I dipped a sterile swab into Pepe's left ear. "That Donovan character was so . . . uncivilized. Imagine . . . using live rabbits to train his dogs! And did you know he once threatened an official, because one of his dogs had been scratched for being too light? Jumped over the rail and grabbed him by the throat. Can you imagine? I'm not surprised Mrs. Augustin reacted the way she did. *I* would certainly be upset if someone was giving drugs to *my* dogs and threatening *me*. She should get a medal for killing Bradley Donovan, not a jail sentence."

I stared at her, a culture dish held motionless out in front of me like an offering plate. I blinked, put the dish on the counter, then reached for the ear drops.

"I really didn't know that about Mr. Donovan," I said, trying to sound disinterested.

"Oh, yes," she said. "Tom cautioned the man about his behavior on several occasions, but it was like talking to a brick wall. I believe Suncoast was going to cancel Mr. Donovan's lease at the end of the season. Of course, now that won't be necessary."

"No, I don't suppose it will," I said. I finished medicating her dog's ears and made a few more notes in the animal's record.

Mrs. Rheems was watching me, a smile fixed on her face like it had been glued there. I didn't know if she expected me to thank her for the backhanded way she was supporting Rachel, or if she was simply waiting for me to pass on any gossip I might have picked up.

"Pepe's ear looks pretty good, Mrs. Rheems," I said, lifting the dog off the table. "As soon as the results of that culture are in, I'll give you a call." I opened the exam-room door and waited for her to get her purse and Pepe's leash.

When she looked back at me, the smile was gone. "Thank you, Miss Holt," she said. She looked disappointed.

I stood in the doorway and watched her as she paid Cynthia. Something about our conversation bothered me, but I couldn't put my finger on it.

At three, while I was cleaning the exam rooms, Dr. Augustin returned. He looked like I felt. He sat down in the lone exam-room chair and rubbed his temples wearily. "The legal system in this state sucks," he said. "How anyone can suspect a ninety-five-pound woman of stabbing a six-foot two-inch man in the chest with a butcher knife is beyond me. I don't care if it *was* her knife." He tipped the chair back and leaned his head against the wall.

I sprayed disinfectant on the exam table and began scrubbing it with a paper towel. "I take it they wouldn't let her out on bail."

"Of course not," he answered. "Like she's really going to skip town or run around stabbing people willy-nilly. Jesus. Matthew agreed to represent her, but the fact that she all but admitted to the police she hated Donovan's guts isn't going to help her defense."

He closed his eyes. "It's partly my fault, I guess. I

encouraged her to tell the police about the phone calls and the drugs, and for the first time in our relationship, she actually listened to me. It figures. Of course, that was before Donovan got himself killed. Now the cops have the weapon *and* a motive for Donovan and at least a motive for Snead's murder."

I hopped onto the exam table. "How is Rachel?" I asked.

Dr. Augustin looked up at me. I could see tiny red veins coursing across the whites of his eyes. I almost asked him if he wanted to go get a beer after work, to talk, but something stopped me.

"She's scared to death. The smell in that place is enough to gag a maggot, and she's in a cell with three other women, all of whom have been there before, evidently." He stood up. "I've *got* to get her out!" He marched over to the doorway, then abruptly turned around. "I need your help, Samantha."

"Jailbreaking isn't one of my specialties," I replied, but immediately regretted saying it.

"I don't mean that," he said, without his usual rancor. "I want you and Frank to snoop around at the track tomorrow. See what you can find out about Donovan. Who his friends were. Who his enemies were. Who might have owed him money. That sort of thing. Russell said he'll be there all day and will try to get you into the kennel compound. I'd go, but you and Frank will look a lot less suspicious. Pretend you're on a date and just wanted to see where the dogs were kept."

I slid off the table. I didn't mind going to the track, but I sure as hell wasn't going with Frank. How could I tell Dr. Augustin that Frank's eyes reminded me of an X-ray machine? "All right," I said, "but I'll take Jeffrey with me. There's a five-K race tomorrow morning that Jeff is planning to run in. Part of the course includes Summerland

Boulevard. If I drive over with him, maybe the two of us can check out the track after the race."

"Thanks, Sam. I owe you one."

About that time Cynthia informed us our next client was waiting. I inhaled deeply and stretched. Having Dr. Augustin back was like a terrible fever breaking. I found I was exhausted, but my headache was better.

"So, aren't you going to say anything about the fact that the clinic didn't burn down in your absence?" I looked at him as we headed into Room 2, hopeful he might apologize for leaving his staff stranded.

Dr. Augustin shook his head, straight-faced, but I could see a faint glimmer in his eyes. "I wasn't worried," he said. "I knew the place was in good hands."

Jeffrey brought chicken in lemon-dill sauce and baked sweet potatoes home that night, enough for four. Miss Priss turned up her nose at the chicken, but ate a hearty portion of potato.

During supper, I told Jeffrey about Rachel and Donovan.

"I have a favor to ask of you," I said, when we had finished eating.

Jeffrey popped open a can of soda and stretched out in the recliner. "You name it," he responded.

"I want you to go with me to the dog track tomorrow, after your race. Dr. Augustin wants me to check around, see if there's anything on Donovan that might help Rachel, and he doesn't want me going alone." I began gathering up our dishes.

Jeff suddenly leaned forward in his chair, grinning. "Sure," he said, "but only if you agree to do something for *me*."

"What?" I asked suspiciously.

"Run in that race tomorrow," he said, then held up his hands in an effort to head off my protests. "I know, I know. You're afraid you'll be last or something. But you won't. This is billed as a 'fun run.' There'll be plenty of people a lot slower than you are. Trust me." He cocked his head to one side. "The T-shirt alone is worth it."

"I'm probably going to regret this, but okay. Just this once."

I didn't have to look to know that Jeffrey was gloating.

CHAPTER 21

•

Sunday, February 27

When Jeffrey failed to make an appearance, I went over to his apartment and pounded on his door.

"Jeffrey!" I called. "You said seven o'clock, so here I am. Now get up." I wrapped both hands around my lukewarm coffee cup and shivered. I was cold and sleepy and not in a very good mood. I had no desire to embarrass myself in front of several hundred people and even less desire to snoop around the dog track afterward.

"Jeffrey!" I shouted. Suddenly his door opened, and I was greeted by a face still wrinkled with sleep.

"Morning," he said sleepily. "I'll be right with you." He smiled, then gently closed the door, leaving me alone on the landing, once again.

"Damn!" I said, and went back in my apartment.

We got to the registration desk just as it was closing. I handed the woman my ten dollars and got a race packet. They were out of T-shirts, she said. Sorry.

Jeffrey and I pinned on our race numbers in silence, then wandered toward the starting line. Everywhere I looked, emaciated bodies in nearly obscene outfits bent, stretched, and bounced up and down on the balls of their feet. I plodded wearily along in my sweats.

"I have to pee," Jeffrey announced, indicating the row of portable toilets that stood like the queen's guard along the side of the road.

"Sure," I said. "See you later."

He cantered off, the muscles of his legs pulsing like finely tuned machinery.

I joined up with a group of less-than-athletic-looking women standing toward the back of the pack. A particularly fat lady in a shocking-pink warm-up suit smiled at me.

"Isn't this exciting?" she asked. "My daughter is up there someplace." She pointed ahead of us. "This is my first race. I've only run three miles twice before, but Becky—that's my daughter—Becky says you always do better than you think you'll do at these things." She looked at me like she expected a response.

"Yes, I guess that's true," I said. "Of course, I'm told you have to be careful not to start out too fast."

"Oh, is this your first race, too?"

I nodded.

"Maybe we could run together," she said. "My Becky says it helps to run *with* someone, and she is so much faster than I am. I told her to go on by herself."

It didn't make any difference to me.

"My name is Elizabeth," the woman said, holding out a fistful of pudgy fingers, their nails encased in fresh acrylic.

"Mine's Samantha," I responded, shaking her hand. We grinned at each other like we were shipmates about to embark on a treacherous voyage to the New World.

The starting gun went off, and a cheer rose from the spectators lining the road. It took several seconds for the mob to begin moving, but slowly a space opened up in front of us, and we started taking tiny steps, then larger ones, until I had to remind Elizabeth to slow down. She was already puffing like a steam engine, and we'd only just passed under the starting banner. The thought of her keeling over before the one-mile mark didn't cheer me up in the least.

But Elizabeth was still puffing away next to me when I heard an official with a stopwatch call out "Ten-ten!" as we turned onto Summerland Boulevard. I felt pretty good, considering I hadn't wanted to be there in the first place.

"If it's okay with you," I said to Elizabeth, "I'm going to pick it up a little."

She smiled weakly and, between gasps, told me to go ahead. Tiny beads of perspiration floated on her makeup, like raindrops on Turtle Wax. I gave her a thumbs-up. She waved.

"Start out at the back," Jeffrey had told me on the way over. "Concentrate on the person directly in front of you. Try to pass him. Then try to pass the next person and so on. Don't think about how fast or how slow you're going, as long as you feel okay. Just watch the guy in front. Make each one you pass a little victory."

I stared at the man running about five yards up. He appeared to be in his sixties, but he looked fit and trim, and I felt particularly victorious when I passed him. I heard him say, "Looking good!" as I went by.

Twelve men and six women later I rounded the turn onto Marlee Road. The finish was just ahead on the west approach to the greyhound-track parking lot. Suddenly I heard Jeffrey call my name. He was standing between two officials who were trying, somewhat unsuccessfully, to keep spectators off the roadway. He was smiling and clapping and pointing at the digital time clock over the finish line. I looked up. It read 25:10.

"Wow," Jeffrey said as I stood off to one side, doubled

over, hands on knees, trying to catch my breath. "What a great finish, Samantha!"

I stood up, still panting. The nausea I felt crossing the finish line was subsiding. "Thanks," I said faintly, then shook my head. "Don't think you're going to get me to run in another race, just because I survived this one."

After we'd gotten something to drink and Jeffrey had eaten three bananas and two containers of yogurt, compliments of a local radio station, we headed across the dog-track parking lot. There were still quite a few cars left and dozens of people wandering around.

I spotted Elizabeth as she came across the finish line. She was hard to miss. She looked like a giant cloud of cotton candy. I didn't feel like chatting. I knew Russell was waiting for us, and I wanted to get the whole sleuthing thing over with. I grabbed Jeffrey's arm and aimed him in the direction of the track. As we crossed Marlee Road another overweight, panting jogger rounded the bend.

"See, you weren't last," Jeffrey said, with an almost straight face. But I noticed he had stepped just out of reach.

Russell had told me to have someone from Security call him up to the kennel compound gate when Jeffrey and I arrived. He was going to try to get us a pass but wasn't optimistic.

Dick Fowley was on duty in his little guardhouse. He was reading the paper and didn't see me walk up.

"Hello, Dick," I shouted through the glass.

He jumped, then slowly got up and opened the door. "May I help you?" he asked, obviously miffed at having someone on foot catch him napping. He eyed Jeffrey and me like we were vacuum-cleaner salesmen.

"Good morning," I said. "Russell Curtis said he'd meet us

here. Would it be possible for you to call and tell him we've finally arrived?"

"Just a minute," he said stonily, and closed the door. He apparently didn't recognize me, and I certainly wasn't going to refresh his memory. I looked at Jeffrey and shrugged.

"Mr. Curtis will be right up," Fowley informed us through the closed door. His voice was muffled. "Please wait over there." He pointed to a grassy knoll several yards away from the compound gate.

"Thank you," I mouthed at him, and Jeffrey and I walked across the roadway.

"Not very sociable, is he?" Jeffrey asked as we waited.

Suddenly Russell's pickup came through the gate. Russell parked on the grass near us and got out.

"Hi, Sam," he said. He smiled at Jeffrey. "You must be Samantha's neighbor. Thanks for helping us out." They shook hands.

"No problem," Jeffrey said. He looked bored.

Russell turned back to me. "They won't give you guys a pass. Everybody's in a tizzy over what happened, and security's tight. I've asked Jimmy Fisher, Donovan's trainer, to join us in the snack bar." He motioned to his truck. "Hop in, and I'll drive you around."

Jeffrey and I slid into the cab, and Russell took off. It was a short trip around to the front of the main building.

"I spoke with Rachel on the phone this morning," Russell said as he pulled into a parking space. "She sounded terrible. She didn't even ask about the dogs, and that's not like her."

The snack bar was located on the ground floor, next to the souvenir shop, which was still closed. I could see tiny greyhound statuettes in a variety of colors and sizes and coffee mugs with the track's logo printed on their sides staring out at me from a display cabinet behind the window.

Inside the snack bar, a lone woman stood behind the counter, reading the Sunday comics and smoking a cigarette. She appeared to be in her late fifties, but it was hard to tell. Her hair was that uniform shade of brown Mother Nature never intended. She was dressed in black trousers, white shirt, and black string tie. Her name tag said SUSAN. She looked up.

"Morning, folks. What can I get you?" Her voice was deep and raspy.

Since Jeffrey and I had left our wallets in my trunk, Russell offered to buy us coffee. He didn't ask if we wanted anything else. There were half-squished jelly doughnuts stacked on a plate under a glass cover, and some kind of Danish that looked about as edible as those plastic creations they put in model homes.

We took our cups to a table as far away from the woman as possible. As we were getting settled a red-haired, freckle-faced young man appeared and came over to our table.

"Thanks for coming, Jimmy," Russell said, shaking the man's hand.

Jeff and I introduced ourselves. The woman behind the counter lifted her coffeepot questioningly, but Jimmy shook his head. "I don't drink coffee, and I've already had my daily quota of Coca-Cola," he told us, pulling up a chair.

"Samantha wants to ask you some questions about Donovan," Russell said. "She's a friend of Mrs. Augustin." He turned to me and added, "No one here thinks Rachel is guilty, either."

I looked at Jimmy. He was about twenty-one or twenty-two, with an open, honest face. I wondered how he could stand to work for someone like Bradley Donovan.

"I really appreciate you taking the time to help us out," I said. "I guess we're here trying to find out who might have wanted Donovan dead. From what I've heard, he isn't . . . wasn't the most popular guy in the world."

Jimmy grinned bashfully, as if he knew I wondered about his relationship with his boss. "No . . . I don't guess he was." He hesitated. "You know, the cops already asked me about Donovan. If he had any enemies. Stuff like that."

"I know. I'm probably going to ask you some of the same questions they did. Sorry. Just bear with me."

He nodded.

"Did he gamble, maybe, or borrow a big sum of money from someone, then not pay it back?"

"I don't think so," Jimmy said. "Brad always seemed to have lots of money, though. He liked clothes. 'Flash and dazzle,' he called it."

"Did you ever see him with anybody you didn't recognize? I mean, more than once or twice?" Mobsters, maybe, I almost added. People with black shirts and white ties and big guns.

Suddenly I wanted to get out of there. I felt stupid and awkward asking a perfect stranger probing questions, like I was some kind of hotshot detective. Dr. Augustin should be doing this, I thought. But I just sat there, hoping I didn't sound as foolish as I felt.

"No," Jimmy was saying. "Just track people. Dog people . . . you know. Or delivery guys from Bayside. And women." He blushed through his freckles and looked down at the table. "Brad went out a lot. With a bunch of different women. Some of them were as old as my mom, some younger than me. Sometimes he brought them to the track. You know the kind." He glanced over at Russell, who nodded and grinned.

I cleared my throat. "Did he seem any different the last month or so? Did he ever appear frightened or worried about anything?"

Jimmy looked surprised. "Yeah, as a matter of fact. He did. He started getting weird calls. By weird I mean the guy on the other end wouldn't say who he was. When I told him Brad was out or busy, he'd act like he didn't know what to do, then hang up. When Brad was there, they'd talk briefly, then Brad would tell me he had to go out. He acted pissed. He'd shove off for a half hour or so. When he got back, he was always up tight." He paused. "I never got up the nerve to ask him what the problem was. He was tough to talk to."

"Did you ever have any idea who the caller might have been? Was it always the same person?"

"I'm pretty sure it was always the same guy," Jimmy said, "but I never did know who it was."

No one said anything. It was awkward. Russell took a drink of coffee and made a face. Jimmy laughed nervously. I'd been putting off asking him about Rachel and Donovan, unable to figure out how to bring it up without mentioning the phone calls or the drugs, but the time had come.

"What did Donovan think of Rachel? I mean, how did he take her trying to start a boycott against Bayside?"

Jimmy shrugged. He was quiet for a few seconds, as if trying to decide how much he should tell me. He looked at Russell, but got no response. Then he drew a deep breath.

"Brad hated Mrs. Augustin. Called her a bitch to her face a bunch of times. Even when other people were around. He never liked her father either." He looked down at his hands. "Brad isn't . . . wasn't really very good with the dogs. Didn't care about them. Not like me. He saw them as expendable. Like a pair of shoes. When they wear out, you throw them away and get a new pair."

He looked uncomfortable, nervous. "He didn't want to pay any more than he had to for food. Or anything, for that matter. Didn't like having to vaccinate them or let them recover from injuries. He was really mad when Mrs. Augustin started complaining about Bayside. Said she was going to wind up costing him a bundle, big time." He paused, looked over at Russell again, then at me. A trace of guilt had crept into his expression. "I was too scared of him to say anything, honest to God. But the meat we were getting from Bayside really wasn't too bad. Not like the stuff they were selling to everyone else."

"Do you think he was meeting someone at Bayside all those times?" I asked.

Jimmy shook his head. "No, he was never gone long enough. Bayside is too far away."

The woman behind the counter spoke up. "You guys want some more coffee?" She held up the pot.

"I don't think so," Russell said, speaking for the group. "But thanks." He looked at his watch. "I've got to be going, Samantha."

"Okay," I said. I looked back at Jimmy. "One last question. Were Donovan and Harvey Snead friendly? I mean, did they know each other very well?"

"You bet. The only reason Harvey got hired on by the track in the first place was because of Brad. He and Harvey's father were friends. Trust me. Harvey Snead was a loser. All he cared about was hanging out at the beach and smokin' dope. Anything to get high." Jimmy wrinkled up his nose in apparent disgust. "It really didn't surprise me, Harvey getting killed. Too bad it was Rachel that got the blame. There were probably a dozen creeps had it in for Harvey for one reason or another."

Russell stood up, and the rest of us followed.

I stuck out my hand. "You've been a big help, Jimmy. Really. Thanks a lot." I smiled. "By the way, what will happen to Donovan's dogs, now that he's gone?"

"Only a few actually belonged to him. He had contracts with half a dozen owners. They'll lease their dogs to other kennels. I guess the few remaining ones will be sold or put up for adoption. I won't let whoever gets his dogs kill them."

"Good for you," I said.

Jeffrey and I thanked Russell, telling him to go ahead, that we'd walk across the parking lot to my car. After he had driven off, however, I started walking back toward the kennel compound.

Jeffrey grabbed my arm. "Uh, Samantha. The car's this way." He pointed over his shoulder.

I kept walking. "I know, Jeffrey, but I want to see how difficult it would be for someone to slip past the guard. Security is supposed to be tight, but Fowley never saw me earlier when I went over to have him call Russell."

"Okay, Sam, but hurry it up, will you? I want to go home and take a shower." He sounded annoyed. I knew it was past his lunchtime.

I patted him affectionately on the arm and trotted across the road to the compound wall. After glancing around to make sure no one was approaching the gate, I moved slowly and what I hoped was nonchalantly toward the guardhouse. When I was about thirty feet away, I stopped.

Fowley was putting what appeared to be a time card into a slot on a rack hanging from the only wall that wasn't glass, the one directly behind his desk. A pickup pulled out of the compound to the right of Fowley's cage and honked. Through the cab window, I saw Fowley wave at the driver, then take out another time card. He made a notation on it, then placed it back on the rack. The truck turned away from me and took off down the road.

I could feel the sweat popping out on my face and neck, dislodging the salt left there during my run. It was a clammy sensation. And my digestive system was working overtime. I held my breath and moved closer. Then Fowley turned around, and I froze. He came over to his chair and sat down. He picked up a magazine and began flipping through its pages, his elbows propped on the desk.

I was starting to get rattled. I tried to tell myself what was the big deal anyway? What would happen if Fowley caught me? Paddle my butt and tell me I was a bad girl? Breathing easier, I continued until I reached the end of the wall. I was barely ten feet from the guardhouse. After a very brief moment that seemed like forever, I slipped around the corner. Fowley never looked up. A few feet back along the inside of the wall, and I was out of sight of the guardhouse altogether. I made the return trip equally unnoticed.

"You were right," Jeffrey said, when I got back across the road. "He never saw you."

I was sweating profusely by that time, but felt strangely exhilarated. "Of course it doesn't really mean anything," I said. "Fowley wasn't on duty when Harvey Snead bought it." But I was smiling.

CHAPTER 22

•

Monday, February 28

First thing that morning I told Dr. Augustin what I learned at the track. He didn't say anything for a minute or so. Then he drew in a deep breath, exhaling it slowly, like a long sigh.

"Well," he said, "it's too bad this Fisher guy wasn't interested enough to follow Donovan. Wasn't he even a little curious about who his boss was meeting?"

I knew Dr. Augustin was disappointed, but his attitude was beginning to irritate me. "Jimmy Fisher is just a kid, for crying out loud." Dr. Augustin looked over at me suddenly. I felt my face grow red, but I went on. "He was scared to death of Donovan. I think he took the job without knowing what kind of person Bradley was and stayed on because of the dogs."

"Kid or not, Jimmy Fisher has given us our only lead so far. If Donovan was never gone more than a short while, maybe someone was meeting him there at the track—an employee or another kennel owner. Or someone from the outside Fisher might not think was unusual. A woman possibly. See what you can find out."

"All right," I said, "but shouldn't the police be doing this? I mean, aren't they better at snooping around, asking questions? Aren't we interfering?"

Dr. Augustin put the dog he'd been working on back in

her cage and closed the door. He turned around and aimed his laser eyes at me. “Probably. But they're convinced Rachel is guilty. That this whole thing is because of some feud between her and Donovan. So what makes you think they're going to try very hard to find the real killer? Matthew has a private detective nosing around, but Rachel can't even afford Matthew, let alone some PI.” He paused and looked away. “She won't take any money from me, of course.”

No, I thought, she wouldn't.

Suddenly, over the intercom, Cynthia's voice announced an emergency. I half expected to see Russell with another one of Rachel's dogs, in spite of the fact that both Snead and Donovan were out of the picture. But it was a cat. When we were through, the intercom came to life again.

“Sam,” Cynthia said, in the speaker's hollow, faintly metallic voice, “Mike is here to see you. I'll put him in Room One.” Dr. Augustin frowned but didn't say anything, and I hurried down the hall.

Michael was waiting for me, looking very Palm Beachy and clutching a bunch of pink carnations.

“I was on my way here and passed one of those cute little bikini-clad flower children.” He stuck out the offering. “I couldn't resist.”

“Thank you, Michael,” I said. “Let's put these on Cynthia's desk so everyone can enjoy them.”

He started to say something, then closed his mouth and followed me up front. Cynthia was busy arranging a similar bouquet in a glass specimen jar.

“Well,” I said. “These will sure brighten the place up, won't they, Cynthia?”

Michael looked slightly embarrassed. “I have some information, Samantha,” he said, after clearing his throat.

"About that little problem we discussed last week." His eyes strayed over to the solitary client sitting in the corner, her toy fox terrier on her knee.

"Okay," I said. "Let's go into Dr. Augustin's office."

Dr. Augustin was at his desk, reading. He looked up and stared at Michael. "I have nothing to tell the press, Mr. Halsey," he said curtly. "About my ex-wife or anything else." He remained seated, his eyes like tiny celestial black holes, sucking the will out of me.

I stood up straight and walked resolutely over to the chair by his desk, pulled it out slightly, then turned to Michael. "Have a seat," I said to him, "and tell us what you've dug up so far." I sat down on the daybed and, with great difficulty, avoided making eye contact with Dr. Augustin.

Michael hesitated. I was smiling at him, trying to appear relaxed, but he didn't move from the doorway. "If Dr. Augustin would rather I—"

"Dug up?" Dr. Augustin asked suddenly. "What are you talking about?"

"Michael volunteered to check out Bayside Meats," I said. "To see if there's some connection between them and Donovan."

Dr. Augustin glowered at me, undoubtedly furious that I'd dare speak to the press. But from his silence, I guessed he was also curious. Rachel's welfare presumably was worth a little consorting with the enemy. I indicated the chair once more.

Michael went over to it and sat down, then took out his little notebook.

"Bayside Meats is run by Stellar Enterprises, Incorporated, a holding company out of Miami," he began, "and managed locally by Mark and Scott Toureau. Stellar bought out the original owners last October. It took some doing, but

I finally discovered that the principal stockholder of Stellar Enterprises is a very wealthy, very powerful Miami businessman.

"According to my source at the *Herald,* most of Stellar's subsidiary companies are legitimate operations. Meat-processing plants mostly, like Bayside, shipping companies, warehouses. A few outfits aren't so legitimate. Those have been involved in everything from income-tax evasion and trafficking in stolen property to money laundering. Our Miami friend has always claimed to have had no knowledge of these activities and so far has never been indicted for anything."

Dr. Augustin didn't move. He had his elbows on the arms of the chair, his fingers forming a little tent over his chest. Watching the two of them, side by side, reminded me of the "Odd Couple." Not that Dr. Augustin was a slob or uncouth, or that Michael Halsey belonged on the cover of *Barron's*. It was just that, until I actually saw them together—Dr. Augustin leaning back in his chair like some streetwise kid from Queens, and Michael, straight-backed in his navy blazer, like he ought to be balancing a cup of espresso on his knee—I never realized how different they were.

"As far as I can tell," Michael continued, "the Toureau brothers have no criminal record, not even a traffic violation. Not locally, anyway. Of course, they haven't been in Florida very long. They're originally from Kansas. Moved here last fall after purchasing Bayside." He shrugged. "Nothing to connect them to Donovan, I'm afraid. Looks like Bayside Meats might turn out to be a dead end." He flipped over a few more pages in his notebook. "Now, Joseph Ames is a different story entirely."

Suddenly Dr. Augustin sat up.

"He's got a record a mile long," Michael said. "Misdemeanors, mostly. Trespassing, disorderly conduct, resisting arrest. And a breaking and entering that got reduced to trespassing. No jail time, other than overnight. Most of his run-ins with the law occurred back in the mideighties. Medical labs, pharmaceutical companies, anywhere they experimented on animals. The medical school over in Tampa." Michael pocketed his notebook.

"Then he apparently switched to abortion clinics. He was arrested in September 1991, during one of those demonstrations at that women's clinic up the road. He doesn't seem inclined toward violence, but he *is* dedicated."

Dr. Augustin was lost in thought for a moment. Then he looked down at his watch and stood up. He seemed unsure about how to act toward Michael. In the end, he offered Michael his hand and attempted a smile. "I appreciate the information, Mr. Halsey. Rachel is innocent. It's important that we find the real killer as soon as possible." He glanced at his watch again, then at me. "Samantha, will you show our first client into a room?" Pleasantries over, he nodded quickly in Michael's general direction and walked out through the lab.

Michael grinned. "I see what you mean about his fondness for the news media." He pushed the chair back over against the desk. "Interesting eyes. If my face had been a piece of sheet metal, they'd have burned right through it."

We walked out to Cynthia's desk. The toy fox terrier had been joined by a Persian cat and a sheltie.

"Thanks, Michael," I said, "for all your help."

"No problem, Samantha. Glad to do it." He paused in the doorway. "Listen, how about dinner Thursday? Casual. I'll pick you up here, around six." I could feel eight pairs of eyes watching me, daring me to say no.

"All right," I said.

"Good. See you Thursday." He winked conspiratorially at Cynthia, then left.

The eyes relaxed.

This is nuts, I thought.

Dr. Augustin took a bottle of aspirin off the pharmacy shelf, opened it, and dumped out three tablets. He put them in his mouth. Without any water, he swallowed. I wondered if he did it just to impress me, the bitter, chalky tablets slowly dissolving at the back of his throat. But his voice was fine.

"I want you to go out to the Ames place and snoop around," he said. "Mr. Ames should be at work. I don't think Mrs. Ames is a problem. Say you've come to check on Bruiser." He started across the hall. "And let me know what you find out so I can call Matthew Kemp."

"When do you want me to do this 'snooping'?" I asked. I was surprised he hadn't suggested I take Frank.

"The sooner the better," he said. "Right now, in fact." He had his hand on the door to Room 1. "P.J. can help me, if it comes to that. She needs the experience, anyway." He went in and closed the door.

Poor P.J., I thought.

CHAPTER 23

•

Joseph and Louisa Ames and their five offspring lived in Oak Grove Manor at the end of a long, narrow, dirt road. Their one-acre lot was nearly hidden from the main thoroughfare by a thick stand of live oak and the remains of an old orange grove. As I drove past the sprawling two-story homes overlooking a perfectly manicured golf course, I wondered how the Ames family could afford to live in such opulent surroundings. When I reached their house, I knew. They had been there first. Or at least their house had.

I pulled up next to Mrs. Ames's beat-up station wagon and switched off the ignition. I stared out at the dilapidated frame house, its wraparound screen porch now devoid of screen. Even a coat of paint wouldn't have helped the view much. The yard was mostly bare dirt. What vegetation there was hadn't seen a lawn mower in years. Rusting wire cages of various sizes were piled up next to the house, along with a tricycle that looked like it had been run over. The front tire was mangled.

I opened my car door and stepped out. A stiff breeze had come up, and tiny dust devils whipped at my ankles, coloring my white uniform a dull shade of beige. I slammed the door and started for the porch.

Suddenly a cacophony of animal voices sounded from

somewhere behind the house. No doubt the alarm system, I thought, because just then a side door opened, and Mrs. Ames stuck out her head. She was holding her youngest. The baby was stark naked.

"Morning," I said cheerily as I approached her. "Dr. Augustin asked me to stop by and see how Bruiser is doing. To save you a trip." If she knew I was lying, she didn't show it. She just stared at me. The baby began to whimper.

"Bruiser is somewhere around here," she said. She looked down at the baby, then back at me. She hesitated a moment before opening the door wider. "Come on in, then, Miss Holt. Little Benji is getting cold with no clothes on."

I stepped up onto the porch and followed her inside. I noticed the door had a crudely constructed pet entrance near the bottom, with a two-way rubber flap over it.

The kitchen, although cluttered and in need of new wallpaper and paint, was clean. A pleasant odor of yeast permeated the air. Two large ceramic bowls, each covered loosely with a towel, sat on the counter. A mound of pale dough lay in a pool of flour on the table.

"Please," Mrs. Ames said, pointing to a coffeemaker sitting next to one of the ceramic bowls, "help yourself. Cups are over the stove. I'll be back in a minute." She and the baby disappeared through swinging doors.

I took down a mug and filled it with coffee. Then I walked over to the sink and looked out the window.

The Ameses' backyard looked like a refugee camp. Scattered among the oaks were several rows of wire cages sitting atop concrete platforms and protected from the rain by sheets of corrugated aluminum. Most of the cages appeared to be occupied. Two large aviaries had been constructed close to the house. Their inhabitants flapped and darted about, piercing the air with raucous whistles and shrieks. An area approximately fifty feet square was enclosed by a chain-link fence. It contained a small makeshift stable and a ready-made aluminum storage shed. A donkey stood quietly in one corner, munching on a pile of what looked like fresh hay.

Everywhere, sparrows and mourning doves pecked the ground, looking for leftovers. Now and then, someone would rattle a cage door or food dish, and the sparrows would rise up like a great dust cloud, then settle back down again.

"All innocent victims, Miss Holt." Mrs. Ames pushed through the double doors and joined me at the sink. She had changed clothes. Instead of the cotton shift she had greeted me in, she now wore a bulky knit pullover sweater and jeans.

"Abused, mostly, or just plain abandoned," she said. "Snakes, birds, ferrets—exotic animals that people try to make pets out of to impress their friends. Then they get tired of them. A few are native Florida species, brought to us after being shot or hit by cars. We have permits for *them*." She looked at me, obvious distrust in her eyes. "We're a legitimate rehab center. I can show you our license, if you're interested."

I took a drink of my coffee. "We haven't seen any of your . . . patients . . . at the clinic, have we?"

Mrs. Ames shook her head. "No. Dr. Samuels takes care of them at his clinic over on Hacienda Drive. As you probably know, he specializes in exotic animals. *He's* really in charge. It's his center. We just let him keep the animals here, after they leave his clinic. Until we can find homes for them, or until someone has the time to drive over to Ocala and let the native ones go." She paused, then looked away.

"We prefer to bring Bruiser to Dr. Augustin," she said, "in

case you're wondering. Dr. Samuels isn't too keen on cats, you see, and Bruiser doesn't get along very well with him."

At that moment we heard a noise and turned around just in time to see Bruiser stick his head through the pet door. I knelt down and called to him. He came in and trotted over to me, chirping and meowing the whole way.

I picked him up. "Oh, Bruiser, you old fleabag, how have you been?" He purred and rubbed his jaw against the side of my face. His ear looked better. I put him down, and he ran over to his food dish and began eating. "His ear is almost completely healed, Mrs. Ames. You've done a terrific job of keeping it clean."

A faint smile appeared on her face. "I try, Miss Holt."

Suddenly the double doors flew open, and the Ameses' four-year-old daughter, followed closely by a younger sister, danced into the kitchen and made straight for Bruiser. The cat grabbed a last mouthful of food, raced across the room, and sailed through the pet door. The little girl stopped abruptly and started to cry.

Mrs. Ames glanced over at me, grinning, and for half a second she looked childlike, innocent. Happy. "Now you see why we can't keep him indoors," she said.

"I certainly do," I said. "Well, I'd better let you get back to your baking. Thank you for the coffee."

I picked up my purse and was headed for the door when the animal alarm went off.

Mrs. Ames's four-year-old blinked away her tears and squealed with delight. "Daddy!" She ran for the door.

I looked at Mrs. Ames. Her eyes flitted from the door to the window to my face like one of her caged birds. The tranquillity I had seen earlier was gone, replaced with a look of uncertainty, even, I felt, a trace of fear.

Suddenly I realized I was trapped there in her kitchen. I

had no idea what to expect from Mr. Ames, but Mrs. Ames didn't look like she intended to back me up in any case. I clutched my purse and tried to think of something believable to say. My mind was a blank.

Mr. Ames opened the door. His daughter flung herself at him, wrapping her arms around his leg. He ignored her. He stood in the doorway and stared at me.

"Hello, Mr. Ames," I said gamely. "I came by to check on Bruiser. I know how busy Louisa is and—"

"No, you didn't," he said.

His voice was so cold I half expected to see icicles stream out of his mouth like Jack Frost nipping at your nose. Except Mr. Ames wouldn't be nipping. Gnawing, maybe. His beard still needed trimming, and he was wearing a flannel shirt instead of a dress shirt and tie. The look on his face reminded me of the men in the movie *Deliverance*. I began hearing banjos in my head.

"You came here to spy," he snarled.

His daughter, probably alerted by the fact that her mother had backed up nearly to the swinging double doors, let go of her father's leg and scurried under the kitchen table to join her sister.

"Dr. Augustin was concerned about Bruiser's ear," I said defensively. "He sent me to see if it had healed properly."

"He sent you to poison Louisa's mind. Turn her against me."

"Nooo, Joseph, really, she d-d-didn't," stuttered Mrs. Ames.

Mr. Ames advanced several steps and peered out of the window, intent on something. He gripped the edge of the sink so tightly his knuckles blanched.

I turned to Mrs. Ames. Then I saw the bruise. The younger Ames girl had made it from the table to her mother and now wanted to be picked up. Mrs. Ames leaned over to lift the child, and her sweater fell away from her neck. A large bluish area started just over her clavicle and appeared to extend all the way across her left shoulder. As she settled her daughter on her hip she saw me staring and quickly pulled up on the sweater. The bruise disappeared.

"You are not welcome here, Miss Holt," said Mr. Ames. His voice had lost some of its edge, and I breathed deeply for the first time in several minutes. "You will leave, now. And tell your boss we will seek medical care for our pet elsewhere in the future."

Mrs. Ames made a sound in her throat like a whimper, but she didn't say anything.

I walked quickly to the door, easing myself around Mr. Ames, who was still staring out the window. "I'm sorry," I said. "Bruiser is a wonderful cat. He deserves the best." I opened the door and hurried out, closing it behind me.

My hands were shaking so hard it took several seconds for me to get my key in the ignition. I lost no time, however, in starting my car and driving off. The dust rose behind me like a curtain.

As I pulled out onto Oak Grove Avenue I realized I was angry more than scared. Angry at Mrs. Ames for letting her husband push her around. Angry at myself for intruding into their personal life. Strangely, I wasn't angry at Mr. Ames. He had a violent temper and needed help, that was obvious. But for some strange reason, I didn't think he was capable of murder.

More than anything, I was angry at Dr. Augustin for sending me to do his dirty work. This whole business with Rachel has gotten completely out of hand, I thought, and I won't be a party to it anymore.

CHAPTER 24

•

Tuesday, March 1

Frank called in sick at five minutes to eight, so P.J. and I had to clean out the kennel. By the time we were finished, I looked like I'd just run in the mutt derby with Mad Max.

Dr. Augustine was furious. None of his surgeries had been worked up by the time he got in, and the place still smelled like dog poop. He yelled at P.J., then apologized profusely when she started to cry. Next, he snapped at me for letting Cynthia schedule so many baths, overlooking the fact that I hadn't even been there the previous afternoon.

"How could *we* know Frank was going to take the day off?" I asked, but Dr. Augustin wasn't in the mood for logic.

"Have P.J. start bathing, and you get busy in the lab." He was headed toward the surgery. He stopped and looked back at me. "And do something about that uniform. You look like you've been mud wrestling."

I wanted to rip out his tongue.

At four, Russell called. He asked for Dr. Augustin. Cynthia was tired of being yelled at for constantly knocking on the exam-room doors with callers who refused to talk to anyone else, so she gave Russell to me.

"Hi, Russell. Dr. Augustin is with a client just now. What's up?"

"Paul Connelly found four of his dogs dead last night."

I held my breath.

"Funny thing is," Russell continued, "they weren't at the track. They were at his home recovering from injuries. After Rachel's house was broken into, Paul hired some fancy security company to install alarms and such. As far as he knows, no one except him has been inside his kennel for over a week."

"Does he have any idea what they died from? I mean, were they acting strange or sick or anything?"

"He said they were fine when he fed them at seven-thirty yesterday morning. Then he went back to the track. When he got home last night, they were dead in their runs."

"He was good about vaccinations, wasn't he? It couldn't have been hepatitis or anything like that, could it?"

"No. Paul never skimped when it came to his dogs. Rachel wouldn't have let him. He did say all four of them had suffered diarrhea and had vomited, though." He paused. "Oh, and one of them had blood all over her mouth and several broken teeth. Like she'd tried to chew her way through the door to her run. All of them looked blue, he said."

"You mean cyanotic?"

"I guess."

"It still might be something infectious," I said. "But it sort of sounds like something toxic, doesn't it? A poison of some kind. I assume he saved the bodies so his vet can do a necropsy."

"I don't know. I'll ask. Tell Dr. Augustin, will you?"

"Sure, Russell, but I don't know what he can do about it. Just keep a close eye on Rachel's house. Maybe you'd better bring us her cats and the dogs she has staying there."

"That's a good idea. I'll do it. Bye, Samantha." He hung up.

When Dr. Augustin came out of Room 2, I told him what Russell had said.

"I think Connelly takes his dogs to Pine Bluffs Animal Clinic," he said. "Call over there and see if we can have some blood and stomach contents from one of those bodies. Frozen is okay. And get hold of Connelly. Ask him for a sample of whatever he fed his dogs yesterday."

"Maybe that's how whoever is responsible made it past his security system," I said.

"It's possible," Dr. Augustin said. "But we're never going to find out unless we get a sample of that food. Now go call Connelly. Please."

He went into Room 1 and shut the door. I headed for the phone in the lab.

According to Paul, all four dogs had eaten chopped beef from Bayside. It was part of an order he'd received a month earlier and had in the freezer there at his house. The kibble and supplements were some he'd been using for a couple of weeks with no problems.

"Do you have any of the beef left?" I asked.

"No," he answered. "And the dogs out at the track are eating an order that came Friday."

"Dr. Augustin wants me to call your vet and see if we can get some blood samples from one of the dead dogs. You go to Pine Bluffs, don't you?"

There was silence on the other end of the line.

"Paul?"

"I didn't save the bodies, Samantha," he said finally. "My trainer took them over to Animal Control early this morning. I wanted them out of there. I was so mad I just didn't think. They're probably ashes by now."

Terrific, I thought. "Okay. No problem," I told him. "But let us know right away if anyone else gets sick."

"Absolutely, Sam. Sorry."

Dr. Augustin shook his head and mumbled "Idiot" under his breath when I told him we wouldn't be getting any samples to analyze. Then he dropped the matter. He seemed a lot less upset about it than I figured he should be. He was probably gloating over the fact that Rachel's boyfriend had screwed up, but that was just a guess.

At six-thirty that evening, after the last client had left, Dr. Augustin and I came into the waiting room and sat down. I kicked off my shoes and began rubbing my left foot in an effort to get some feeling back in my toes. Dr. Augustin rested his head against the wall and stretched out his legs. They were long, like Jeffrey's, but shaped better.

"God, what a day," he said.

"Yes," I agreed. "I never thought I'd miss Frank, but I sure did today."

Dr. Augustin looked over at me. "Oh, Frank is okay. He just needs to choose his friends a little better. And settle down, instead of partying all the time. I expect that's what happened to him last night. When he left here, he said he was headed for the beach." Dr. Augustin sat up. "By the way, what did you find out at the Ames place?"

I shook my head. "Not much. Mrs. Ames was very nice. The two of them run a wildlife rehab center in their backyard. With Dr. Samuels. There are cages filled with animals scattered all over the place. Everyone looks well cared for, including Bruiser. I didn't see anything suspicious. No greyhounds or anything." I paused.

Dr. Augustin stared at his shoes—Nike lightweight hiking boots.

"Mr. Ames is a violent man," I said. "I think he beats Mrs. Ames."

Cynthia looked up, suddenly.

"He came home while I was there yesterday, and Louisa was scared shitless. Probably about me being there. She has huge bruises on her neck and shoulders. She tried to cover them up, but I saw them, anyway."

Dr. Augustin narrowed his eyes and frowned.

"He accused me—us—of spying on them," I continued. "Said I was there to turn Louisa against him. I thought for a second he was going to hit her or me, but he managed to get a hold of himself. Told me to tell you they'd find someone else to take care of Bruiser from now on."

Dr. Augustin shook his head. "I can't say I'm disappointed they won't be back. I'll miss Bruiser, but I sure as hell won't miss the rest of that family." He looked over at me and smiled faintly. "Thanks for checking them out, Sam. I'm sorry about Ames. I really didn't expect him to be there or I never would have asked you to go."

"That's okay. I guess." There wasn't much point in holding a grudge.

"So, what do you think?" he asked. "Is Ames a murderer or just your garden-variety lunatic?"

"Ames may use his wife as a punching bag," I said, "but he obviously cares about those animals he keeps there. Even Bruiser. So I don't think he could drug a dog just to make a point." I shook my head. "No, I don't think he's capable of premeditated murder. Manslaughter, maybe, in a fit of rage, but that's all."

Suddenly Cynthia popped up from behind her desk. "I'm finished here," she said. "It was a good day, to say the least." She turned off the computer and reached inside the supply closet for her coat. "See you Thursday." She threw me a look that said, "Be careful!" then picked up her purse and the night-deposit envelope.

"Thursday it is," said Dr. Augustin.

I winked at her.

After she left, Dr. Augustin locked the door and turned over the "Closed" sign. He came back to his chair and sat down, lacing his fingers behind his head. "I still don't trust Ames," he said. "But there are a couple of other strong possibilities we need to look into." I turned my head, and his eyes locked onto mine like radar tracking devices. "What are you doing tomorrow morning?"

I drew a complete blank. "Nothing. Laundry, I guess. Whatever." I should have known, should have been prepared.

He smiled. "How would you like to visit Bayside Meats with me?"

"Gee, I don't know—" I started.

"Come on, be a sport, Samantha." He paused. "I'd really like you to come along." His eyes were so black, so limitless.

"I guess so. Sure, why not?"

"Great! I'll pick you up at your place after I finish doing treatments. Or maybe you'd like to come in and help me." He was grinning then, and I could feel his eyes losing their grip.

"Forget it," I said. "Pick me up at nine. For once, *you* can give Mad Max his allergy medication."

Dr. Augustin laughed, and we went back to the kennel in search of Charlie.

I don't know. It seemed I was bent on self-destruction.

CHAPTER 25

•

Wednesday, March 2

Dr. Augustin honked at me from the parking lot behind my apartment building. His casual manner irritated me. I was already mad at myself for agreeing to go with him. Oh well, I thought, at least he didn't suggest I make the trip alone this time.

I hurried down the steps and across the lawn to his Jeep. As I slid into the front seat I noticed he made no effort to hide his approval of my outfit. I'd worn a fitted denim skirt that extended several inches below my knees, a pale rose, long-sleeve cotton blouse, and leather boots. Long skirts and shoes with heels always made me feel thinner somehow.

He was dressed in black twill slacks and a yellow pullover shirt that made his skin appear even darker than it already was. The muscles of his shoulders and arms strained against the confines of the knit material.

"So, what are you planning to say once we get there?" I asked him after we were under way. "I mean, you certainly can't tell them the *real* reason we're paying them a visit."

He chuckled. "Oh, I'll think of something. Just go along with me, Samantha. Toss around that mane of yours and smile a lot. But keep your eyes and ears open."

• • •

Bayside Meats was located, not on the bay, but out in the unincorporated boonies on a piece of pastureland once intended as an industrial park. Unfortunately for the original developers, the main highway took an alternate route. Apparently, Bayside was it, at least for the present.

After thirty minutes of bumper-to-bumper traffic, Dr. Augustin turned onto Marine Drive. It was a narrow but well-maintained service road that wandered through scrub and palmetto before finally ending up at Bayside's doorstep. He drove through the open gate and parked next to a door with the words BAYSIDE MEATS, INC. stenciled on it. WHOLESALE ONLY. OPEN M-FR, 7:00–3:00.

The building was a long, plain, two-story aluminum structure painted white. Other than the door at the entrance, there were two enormous garage doors, both closed, and no windows. Five cars and three delivery-type trucks were parked along the south side of the building. One of the trucks had BAYSIDE MEATS—QUALITY PET FOOD SINCE 1971 and two telephone numbers painted in yellow on its side panels.

Except for the vehicles, the place looked deserted. Dr. Augustin and I walked up the steps to the door, and he tried the knob. It was locked.

"They must not get many walk-ins," I said.

Dr. Augustin rapped loudly on the door. "Well, someone's here. Either that or they've converted the parking area to a used-car lot."

Suddenly a female voice spoke to us from a small intercom speaker located over the door. "Yes?"

"We're here to discuss a meat contract with Mr. Toureau," Dr. Augustin said. "We don't have an appointment. I didn't think one would be necessary."

"Just a moment," said the voice. I felt someone's eyes

studying us from the other side of the door, but couldn't see any peephole or camera anywhere. Then we heard the doorknob click. Dr. Augustin tried it again, and this time the door opened. We stepped inside.

The reception area was attractively done in Danish modern, with blond wood and steely-blue carpeting. Pictures of greyhounds and exotic cats, some posing in a circus setting, adorned the walls. A large glass-and-chrome display case was filled to overflowing with bags and cans of pet food and bottles of vitamins and fluid replacement and flea dip.

A young, well-endowed brunette in a white tube top and red leather skirt sat behind a large desk chewing gum and pushing a wooden stirrer around in a half-full mug of coffee. The mug proclaimed its owner to be THE WORLD'S BEST SECRETARY.

"Mr. Toureau is busy right now," she said. "If you'd like to take a seat, he'll be back shortly." She smiled vacantly and snapped her gum.

There weren't any papers on her desk, and I didn't see any in-box anywhere. A pink telephone memo pad, a telephone, a copy of *People* magazine, and the coffee mug were the only blemishes on an otherwise pristine work surface. No typewriters, no file cabinet, nothing, in fact, to indicate anything of a secretarial nature ever took place there.

Dr. Augustin and I sat down in the lone reception chairs. To our left was the front door. To our right was what appeared to be a bathroom. The door was open a few inches, and I could see a sink faintly illuminated by the ceiling fixture in the reception area. On the way to the bathroom and set in the wall behind Dr. Augustin and me was another door that apparently had a glass panel in it. The panel was covered by a large piece of black poster board. One corner had come loose, and I could see light behind it.

"Is there a bathroom my associate could use?" Dr. Augustin asked the world's best secretary.

I looked at him blankly.

"Sure," she said. "Over there." She pointed to the room with the sink, then opened up her magazine.

Dr. Augustin inclined his head toward the door with the poster board. When I didn't move, he took hold of my arm and pushed me up.

Just then the telephone rang. Still gazing at her magazine, the girl picked up the receiver. "Bayside," she said.

I hurried over to the bathroom, pulled the door closed, then went for the door with the poster board. It was unlocked. I glanced over my shoulder at the girl. She was busy scratching something down on her memo pad and popping her gum. I hesitated a fraction of a second. Dr. Augustin nodded his head encouragingly, so I opened the door and stepped through, closing it behind me.

The stench that hit me was incredible. It was the smell of rotting flesh. As if I'd suddenly stepped into the bowels of a dinosaur that was in the process of decomposing.

I was standing on a platform several feet above the floor of the warehouse. To my right was an eight-foot high mound of dark red meat cut into various-sized chunks. Each chunk appeared to be dusted with charcoal. Blood emanated from the mound and ran in streams all over the floor and down a drain hole set in the center of the room. Two men in rubber boots were using coal shovels to scoop up the chunks and feed them into some kind of grinding machine, which spewed maroon-colored bits out into a giant white tub. I swallowed and looked away.

To my left was a large walk-in freezer. The door was

open, and fog clouds drifted out like small ghosts, then slowly disappeared. Next to the freezer was a long, low room—almost a building within a building. It had a single door and no windows. Two very large, extremely muscular men lounged against the wall outside the door. They were holding guns. Big guns. I reached for the doorknob behind me just as three men came out of the room. Two of them were dressed in suits and carried briefcases. The third man was dressed in a black turtleneck and jeans.

I turned around, opened the door, and rushed back inside. The girl at the reception desk saw me, and a look of confusion and fear totally transformed her face. She jumped up from her desk, turning over her coffee mug.

I tried to smile. "I got lost," I said. "I thought this was the bathroom. Sorry." I quickly headed for the real bathroom. I felt sick. Once inside, I stared at my reflection in the mirror. What the hell is going on in this place, I asked myself, that they need armed guards? I splashed water on my face, then dried it with a paper towel. I'd left my purse on the floor next to Dr. Augustin. Without blush, I looked pale and drawn. I pinched my cheeks to get some color back in them and opened the bathroom door.

The man in blue jeans was talking to Dr. Augustin. The receptionist still looked a little flustered as she tried to clean up the puddle of coffee on her desk. She glared at me.

"This is my assistant, Miss Thompson," Dr. Augustin said, smiling broadly. "Samantha, this is Mark Toureau."

Mr. Toureau turned around and proceeded to visually undress me. He had light brown hair, intense green eyes, and a neatly trimmed beard with just a hint of gray sprinkled through it. The overall effect was incredibly sexy, despite the sleazy look his eyes gave me.

"How do you do, Miss Thompson," he said, sticking out

his hand. "Mr. DiAngelo has been telling me about his plans for a mini-zoo."

"Mr. Toureau," I said, "thank you for seeing us. We've heard so much about Bayside." Reluctantly, I shook his hand. I noticed that Dr. Augustin was staring at me, his smile slowly dissolving. I realized, too late, that he undoubtedly meant for me to keep my mouth shut and let him do the digging.

"Oh? And who has been spreading nasty rumors about us?" Mr. Toureau was grinning playfully, but I thought I detected a note of concern in his voice.

"Only good things, of course," I said, trying to sound like my head was two thirds fluff. His kind of woman, if the girl in red and white was any example.

Mr. Toureau relaxed visibly. "We *do* try our best," he said. "Now, Mr. DiAngelo, tell me how Bayside can help you."

I was a memory. I sat down.

Dr. Augustin crossed his arms and leaned against the wall. "We're interested in providing our carnivores with the latest in formulated diets, Mr. Toureau. Meat, of course, but supplemented with vitamins, minerals, and fatty acids. The usual. Can you provide such a diet? Say, one or two hundred pounds a week to start?"

Mr. Toureau frowned and ran his fingers through his beard. "Formulated diets for exotic carnivores are expensive, Mr. DiAngelo," he said.

Dr. Augustin nodded. "Cost is a factor, certainly, but the health of these endangered animals is of the utmost importance. Our backers want only the best." He smiled benignly, and I saw that the receptionist was eyeing him. The hormones circulating in this room must be phenomenal, I thought with some amusement.

Toureau seemed to be considering this. "Let me look into it," he said finally. "I'll give you a call sometime next week."

Dr. Augustin straightened up. "Terrific," he said. "I'll fax you a list of what I need." He glanced around. "You *do* have a fax, don't you?"

"Yes, of course." He looked at the receptionist. "Gretchen, give Mr. DiAngelo our fax number, would you?" He turned back to Dr. Augustin and offered his hand. "It certainly was nice to meet you."

"Yes," said Dr. Augustin. "I hope we can do business." He shook Toureau's hand.

Toureau winked at me, then left through the door with the cardboard curtain. I got up. Gretchen, her pouty mouth and chest thrust as far forward as was physically possible, handed Dr. Augustin one of her pink memo slips. He took it. Then he went over to the door, opened it, and waited for me to pass through. He pulled the door closed behind us, and I heard the lock click into place.

"DiAngelo?" I asked, after we'd gotten into his Jeep.

"My mother's maiden name," he said. He started the engine and pulled out onto Marine Drive. "Do you get the feeling Mr. Toureau isn't particularly interested in doing business with us?"

"Maybe he isn't in a position to provide special diets for zoo animals."

"What do you think all those circus animals pictured on his walls are?" I didn't say anything. "What did you see on the other side of that door? When you came back, you looked like you were about to puke."

"I was," I said. "You should see how they process the meat in that place." Then I told him about the guns.

"Well, now, isn't *that* interesting?" he said.

"What are you going to do?"

"I don't know yet. I'll have to think about it."

Well, *I* sure didn't have to think about it. I absolutely, positively refused to have anything more to do with Rachel's problem or "case" or whatever Dr. Augustin wanted to call it. And that was *that*!

CHAPTER 26

•

Thursday, March 3

Dr. Augustin avoided any mention the next day of Bayside Meats, the armed thugs, *or* Rachel. It was almost as if I'd imagined the whole thing. I didn't even tell Cynthia. Trouble was, Dr. Augustin spent the entire morning humming to himself and being nice. Even P.J. was worried.

"What's gotten into *him*?" she asked me as we ate our lunch. Cynthia was at her post, and Dr. Augustin had gone home until three.

"Who cares?" I said. "Let's just enjoy it while it lasts." But I figured Dr. Augustin was up to something. He was always in a good mood when things were going his way. Of course, since things hadn't actually been going our way of late, he must've known something *I* didn't know. The question was, what?

At 3:10, Mr. Meyerson arrived with Missy. I was prepared for a confrontation between him and Dr. Augustin. But from his expression and the fact that he wouldn't look any of us in the eye, I guessed he was feeling a little guilty. After all, Dr. Augustin *had* saved Missy's leg, not to mention her life.

"How's she been doing?" I asked Mr. Meyerson as I checked the splint on Missy's left rear leg. The little dog whined and licked at my hand.

"Pretty good," he said. "She's a real trooper, considering everything."

When Dr. Augustin came into the exam room, Mr. Meyerson sprang to his feet. "Dr. Augustin, I want to apologize for last Thursday night," he exclaimed. "The commission meeting. I don't know what came over the wife and me. That Ames fellow had us convinced we would be helping the community. You know . . . doing what was right."

He was talking fast, and his voice was getting louder. I went over to the door and gently closed it.

"I've never even *been* to the dog track," he continued. "What do *I* know?" He sat down again.

I felt kind of sorry for him.

Dr. Augustin finished writing in Missy's file and turned around.

"Then Mrs. Augustin said someone had been drugging her dogs," said Meyerson, his voice a little softer, "and that's why they were attacking people. When I confronted Ames after the meeting, he said she was lying to protect her own interests, but I didn't believe him." He cleared his throat. "Please tell your wife I'm sorry."

Dr. Augustin came around the table and put his hand on Mr. Meyerson's shoulder. "Don't give it another thought, Carl. Ames is good at conning people. Especially people like you and your wife—people with good intentions." He took his hand away. "I'll tell Rachel what you said. She'll understand."

Mr. Meyerson looked relieved. He got up, transferring Missy to his left arm, and held out his hand. "Thanks . . . for everything."

"You bet," said Dr. Augustin. He shook Meyerson's hand.

"See you and Missy in a couple of weeks. You're doing a great job with that splint, by the way."

I walked Mr. Meyerson out to the reception desk. Cynthia handed me a slip of paper. It had Michael's work number on it.

"Call him when you get a chance," she said. "He'll be at his desk until four. He said it was important." She had that rapturous look on her face again.

I went to the hall extension and slowly punched in Michael's number, trying to gather my thoughts together. I'd completely forgotten about our date.

He picked up on the first ring, as if he'd been hovering over the telephone, waiting for me to call. "Halsey," he said.

"Michael, it's Samantha."

"Golly, it's good to hear your voice, Samantha. Listen, I'm really sorry to do this to you at the last minute, but I'm going to have to cancel our dinner date. I'm supposed to cover some big shindig over at the University of South Florida tonight. Believe you me, if I could get out of it, I would." He sounded sincere. "How about tomorrow night?"

"Tomorrow would be fine," I said. I was relieved about not having to discuss Bayside or Rachel or Joseph Ames with him.

"Terrific! Same time tomorrow, then?"

"Sure, Michael, six o'clock."

"I've missed you, Samantha." His voice was wistful, and suddenly I felt guilty, because I hadn't missed him at all. Hadn't even thought about him since Monday. Not that I'd had much time to, of course.

"Me, too," I lied.

"Well, until tomorrow."

"Bye, Michael." We hung up.

I stood in the hall for a few moments, wondering how I'd

gotten myself into another one-sided relationship, even if it *was* the other way around this time. Then Dr. Augustin called me into the exam room, and Michael, once again, slipped away.

We finished up at 5:30. Frank had requested the afternoon off, and I'd agreed to feed everyone and let the dogs out in the backyard one last time before going home. As I was fighting with Mad Max, trying to get him back in his run, I realized Dr. Augustin was standing in the kennel doorway.

"You could have lent me a hand here," I said.

He ignored me. "I just got finished talking to Russell," he said. "Three of Rachel's dogs are scheduled to race tonight. He's pretty excited. She hasn't had an entry since the night Donovan was killed."

I closed the door to Max's run and went over to the sink to wash the slobber from my hands. "Do you think they'll be okay, now that Snead is gone?"

"Hopefully. I can't see why anyone would care about Rachel's dogs now that she's in jail. They've accomplished what they set out to do—get her out of the way. She was obviously poking around where she shouldn't have been." He began checking the animals, one by one. When he got to the end of the row, he stopped. "Want to go see the dogs run tonight?"

I dried my hands. Dr. Augustin was humming and scratching Charlie's head. The cat lay sprawled out on the shelf where the food dishes were kept, waiting for his dinner. I made a point of fumbling with the various containers of food, trying to distract Dr. Augustin so I could think. My actions started a chorus of barking and meowing, but instead of yelling for quiet, like he usually did, Dr. Augustin just stood next to the sink, petting Charlie.

Well, I thought, there's no reason to believe he's asking me out on a date. It has to be something else . . . something to do with Rachel. He wants me to play detective again. I ground my teeth. On the other hand, maybe Rachel wants him to watch out for Russell. After all, it *is* the guy's first time running the dogs since her arrest. That's probably it.

"Okay," I said finally. "If you promise to help me do treatments."

"Later," he said, smiling. "This shouldn't take long. We can do treatments when we get back."

Now why do I suddenly have a bad feeling about this? I asked myself.

CHAPTER 27

•

I went home to change and feed my cats. I found a box of roses and a note from Michael waiting on the landing by my door.

Sorry about tonight. Be good. Love, Mike. I hoped the florist had added the *Love* part.

At seven, I drove back to the clinic and found Dr. Augustin pacing around in the reception area. He glanced at his watch.

"The first race is at seven-thirty, Samantha. I told Russell we'd be there."

He ushered me out and locked the door. He was antsy about something, but I had to admit, I preferred him that way. The low-key Mr. Nice Guy demeanor didn't suit him.

Dr. Augustin paid our way in and bought me a program. The rows of numbers and abbreviations after every dog's name looked like hieroglyphics to me.

"How am I going to win any money if I can't even read the program?"

"I'll explain it to you later," he said. "First, let's find Russell."

We walked past the snack bar crowded with people, some with small children in tow, ordering hot dogs, popcorn, and ice cream. I suddenly realized I was hungry, but didn't say anything. Dr. Augustin seemed particularly focused at that moment.

Russell was waiting for us at the weigh-in area. I watched as race officials checked the ear tattoos on a group of eight greyhounds, each one saddled with a race blanket bearing a large number.

"Domino Joe," Russell said, pointing to the number-two dog, dressed in blue. "He's drawn a good starting position for the second race. Keep your fingers crossed."

I grinned. "Should I risk a couple of dollars on him?"

"Absolutely," Russell said. "To show, at least." Then he turned to Dr. Augustin and lowered his voice. "The executive offices are closed, and everyone's gone home. The cleaning crew should be finished up and out of there by eight."

"What do you mean 'the executive offices are closed'?" I asked Russell, my tone accusatory, as well as a tad fearful.

Russell looked first at Dr. Augustin, then back at me. His expression was one of confusion. "I assumed you came along to help," he said.

"Help do what?" I glared at Dr. Augustin, steeling myself.

"You and I are going on a little fact-finding expedition," he said. "Something felonious is obviously taking place out at Bayside. It got Harvey Snead and Bradley Donovan killed. Rachel was threatening to expose it, and now she's in jail. Don't ask me why, but I think Thomas Rheems is involved. I don't trust his wife. And Rheems showed up at Suncoast about the time this meat problem started. It might be a coincidence, but I don't think so."

"You lied to me," I said. "You never intended to watch the races, did you? You conned me into coming along because you knew I'd say no if you came right out and told me what was up, didn't you?" I was really mad, and Dr. Augustin knew it.

He backed away. "I never lied to you, Samantha. Rachel *does* have three dogs running tonight. Listen. If you don't want to help me, you don't have to. You can go down there"—he inclined his head in the direction of the spectator area—"and watch the races while I see what I can find in Rheems's office." He stepped closer. "Only, I wish you'd come along. I could really use your help." He paused. "I need you, Samantha," he said, lips tight, as if he'd just bitten down on something sour.

We were interrupted by the cheering of the crowd. I turned around in time to see eight wasp-waisted creatures fly past me in a flurry of sand, legs, and color. They were in pursuit of a small white object that looked more like a dust mop than a rabbit. It was attached to a mechanical arm that sped around the inside of the track, periodically flicking out sparks as it went. The dogs, of course, never caught up. In just over half a minute, the lure escaped down into a pit, with the dogs piling up around it, barking excitedly. Leashes ready, the leadouts ran to retrieve their charges.

"Well?" Dr. Augustin asked, after the crowd had quieted down.

"What if we get caught?" I asked him.

"We're not going to get caught. Trust me. Do you see any armed thugs around anywhere? As a matter of fact, do you see any guard under the age of sixty-five? The only areas the track is concerned about are the betting windows."

I took two dollars out of my jeans pocket and handed them to Russell. "Here. Put this on Domino Joe. To win." He took the money, smiling. Then I looked up at Dr. Augustin. "Let's go," I said. "Before I change my mind."

• • •

The executive offices of the Suncoast Kennel Club were on the third floor, just beneath the ritzy Derby Pavilion Restaurant. Russell said an elevator automatically went from the ground floor to the Pavilion, without stopping in between, unless you had a key. There was an interior fire escape that went up the opposite side of the building, with an exit on each floor. You had to get past security, but that wouldn't be difficult, he said.

We made our way through the throngs of people milling about near the betting windows, drinking beer, and watching the little closed-circuit TV screens that clung to massive concrete pillars throughout the area. The image duplicated on each TV was a replay of the first race.

At the far side of the building, we spotted a guard. He was leaning against the wall, apparently working on that day's crossword puzzle. His walkie-talkie clicked and clacked and uttered an occasional garbled message, presumably intended for someone else, since he ignored it.

The stairwell was about twenty feet to the man's right. Dr. Augustin grabbed my sleeve to slow me down.

"Let's wait until the start of the next race, which is in"—he glanced over his shoulder at the odds board—"four minutes. I'm betting that guy will get distracted by the race and never notice us."

As the mechanical arm began its swing around the far side of the racecourse, people seated on the wooden benches down by the track stood up. Those already standing back near the beer pulls turned their attention to the TV screens. Dr. Augustin and I moved closer to the fire escape. As predicted, when the dogs left the starting box, the guard looked over at them. I tried to see where Domino Joe was in the melee, but couldn't.

The noise from everyone urging on their favorites was deafening. It hid the scrape of the hinges as Dr. Augustin pulled open the heavy metal door. We entered the stairwell, unnoticed, then quickly climbed to the third-floor landing. Dr. Augustin peered through the little glass window in the door.

"The hall lights are still on," he whispered, "but I don't see anyone." He glanced down at his watch. "It's just eight."

He extracted two pairs of surgical gloves from his jacket pocket and handed me one pair. I put them on. Then Dr. Augustin drew two gum balls from his other pocket and held out his hand. "Good for the nerves," he said, smiling.

His apparent nonchalance about breaking into a building in the presence of several thousand people only compounded my nervousness. Chewing gum was not about to calm me down. I declined, so he popped both pieces into his mouth. Then he slowly pushed open the door, and we started down the hall.

Finding Rheems's office was a snap. A large reception area, with a receptionist's desk, several very comfortable-looking chairs, and two glass cases containing a myriad of greyhound figurines and racing memorabilia was located at the end of the hall near the elevator. There were four doors along the wall immediately behind the reception desk, all closed. According to the little bronze nameplates beside each door, the office on the far right belonged to Thomas Rheems, Asst. General Manager.

Dr. Augustin tried the door. It was locked. He removed a small box from his back pocket, opened it, and took out a long, thin surgical knife, one I had never seen him use before. He very carefully inserted the tiny blade into the lock, pulled up on the doorknob, then rotated the blade a fraction of a turn. After three tries, I heard a faint click, and the door opened. Dr. Augustin looked almost priggish and whispered, "See, nothing to it."

Dr. Augustin's talents were many, to be sure, but I'd never realized until right then that they included burglary. I swallowed, but there wasn't a trace of saliva anywhere in my mouth. It was too late to ask for a piece of gum. With a feeling of impending doom, I waited as he ran his hand along the inside wall, located a switch, and turned on the overhead lights.

The interior of Rheems's office was done in mauve and gray. The plush carpeting was obviously new, as was the leather-and-oak furniture. Nowhere in the room did I see a single greyhound—not on the desk, not depicted in any of the reproductions decorating the walls, nowhere. And there was nothing of a personal nature either—no photos on the credenza, no diplomas or certificates of appreciation. It was almost as if no one occupied the office at all.

Dr. Augustin began opening desk drawers and rifling through their contents.

"What exactly are we looking for?" I whispered as I slid back one of the doors to the credenza.

"I don't know. Anything that looks suspicious or relevant. Letters to or from Bayside Meats or anyone associated with Stellar Enterprises. Correspondence with Donovan. Financial reports that might indicate an unusual expenditure or income involving any of them."

I located a file drawer in the credenza and pulled out a folder labeled *B. J. Donovan Kennels, Inc.* I handed it to Dr. Augustin.

"There's a file on each kennel leasing space here, including one for Red Cavalier Kennels."

I watched as he flipped through the sheaf of papers. From the scowl on his face, I gathered that the file contained nothing useful. He handed it back to me, and I continued my search.

Dr. Augustin was working on the bottom drawer to Rheems's desk when I heard him chuckle. "Well, well, well. What have we here?" He was staring at a sheet of paper he'd apparently found under a pile of *Boater's World,* which he had scattered about on the floor.

I abandoned the credenza and peered over his shoulder. "What is it?" I asked.

"Appears to be a shipping schedule for Hector Miranda Limited, a Costa Rican freight company operating out of Puerto Limón. Most of the destinations are here in Florida—Tampa, Miami, Jacksonville. Someone has circled the arrival dates for the port of Tampa." He handed me the paper. "Under 'cargo' they've listed textiles, bananas, coffee, and beef."

"That awful stuff I saw them grinding up into dog food came from Costa Rica? Why not use Florida meat? Aren't we supposed to be a big cattle producer? Or why not Nebraska or Texas? It's got to be cheaper than shipping it all the way from Central America." I gave the schedule back to him.

"I'm sure it would be, if dog food was all they were importing."

I stared at him. His face had taken on a childlike impishness. "What do you mean?" I asked.

"Drugs, Samantha. Cocaine. Probably hidden in frozen blocks of chopped beef. Think about it. The USDA doesn't have to check it, except superficially, because it's already decharacterized and earmarked for Bayside." He spotted a copy machine in the corner of the room and headed for it. "And it's coming from Costa Rica. Beef is a big export item there. U.S. Customs is understaffed and overworked. Remember those bananas that came from Colombia a couple of years ago? The ones with the coke buried in the bottom of the boxes. *That* shipment made it all the way to the supermarkets before anyone discovered it. Dogs, of course, would be next to useless. The odor of the meat would confuse them."

He turned on the copier. In the deserted office suite, it sounded like a jet plane warming up. I glanced nervously toward the door, then back at Dr. Augustin. After a few seconds he fed the paper into the machine, waited for it to come out the opposite end, then retrieved it and his copy.

"We don't have any proof, of course," he said, flicking off the machine.

An image of the two of us sneaking past the armed bodybuilders at Bayside flashed in my head, and I shivered. Dr. Augustin appeared determined to get himself killed, and for some reason, I was being sucked right along with him.

"Too bad we didn't get any samples of meat from Connelly's place," he said. "My bet is his dogs got a sample of the goods in one of Bayside's shipments to Connelly's kennel. Bag probably broke open in transit or when they thawed it out. They didn't notice it when they ground the stuff up."

Suddenly Dr. Augustin motioned for me to keep quiet. He made his way across the room and stopped at the wall just to the right of the door, listening. I quickly followed him. When I opened my mouth to ask what was wrong, he put his finger to his lips and pointed in the direction of the hallway. Then I heard them—two people talking, a man and a woman. They were approaching Rheems's office from the elevator. Once in the reception area, they stopped.

"Tom is getting cold feet," said the woman. I bit my lip. It was Sylvia Rheems talking. "If he finds out about you and

Donovan, he'll quit for sure, wash his hands of the whole thing. Then where will you and your little operation be?"

"He won't find out. I made certain nobody ever saw the two of us together, you know that."

I felt Dr. Augustin's body tense, and he stopped chewing his gum. He'd apparently recognized the man's voice. I, too, found it familiar, but I wasn't thinking very well and couldn't quite put a face to it.

"Donovan was a fool," the man continued, "sending Harvey Snead out to that Augustin woman's house. She wasn't about to go to the police about the drugs. But robbery is another matter entirely. He pushed her too far." The man coughed, then cleared his throat. "Tom could've worked something out to shut her up. But nooo . . . Brad had to try thinking for himself. What an idiot." He paused. "I had no alternative. He was a liability. And a greedy SOB."

"Still . . . murder wasn't part of the deal. This wasn't supposed to be any big thing where people get killed. Nothing is worth murder." The woman's voice had become shrill, pleading.

"Keep your voice down, Sylvie, for God's sake!" the man hissed.

They had moved across the reception area and now stood quite near the door leading into Rheems's office. We were so close, I imagined Sylvia and her companion could hear my breathing, smell Dr. Augustin's bubble gum. I froze.

"Listen, I want you to do something for me," the man said. "I want you to go back to that five-thousand-square-foot mansion you have out on that little private sandbar and look out at the end of your own personal dock at that nice motor sailer Tom has parked there and then think about what you just said."

His voice was deep and throaty, filled with menace. I heard the woman start to cry. Suddenly his voice softened.

"Sylvie, we never had anything nice when we were growing up. You always said that when you got married, you wanted a guy could buy you a big house and diamonds and a slick sports car. Well, now you have them. Surely you don't want to throw that away." Silence. "Well, do you?"

Sylvia blew her nose. "I guess not," she said through the tissue. "It's just that Tom is so nervous, it rubs off. He's not strong like you. And with Rachel Augustin almost bringing the health department or whoever in to sniff around . . ."

One of them leaned against Rheems's door, causing it to rattle, and my heart missed a cue, then began racing wildly. Dr. Augustin never twitched.

"Rachel Augustin is safely out of the picture." The man paused, and I heard the click of a cigarette lighter. "All of the evidence points to her as Donovan's killer. Snead's, too, although Donovan may be fingered for that one. It doesn't make any difference. She's got more to worry about now than dog food."

"What about Rachel's husband? The veterinarian?" Sylvia asked.

"What about him?"

"I did what you asked. Went to his clinic, talked around. The girl he has working for him acted like she barely knew Rachel, let alone anything important." Dr. Augustin glanced down at me and winked.

"So what are you worried about? Augustin is an asshole. Always poking around in other people's business. Nobody ever pays any attention to him. He's a sideshow, a clown." That time Dr. Augustin twitched. Actually, it was more like a seizure.

"I've got to go." This from Sylvia. "Tom and the others

are waiting downstairs. They'll think I fell through or something."

"Yeah, sure. Listen, Sylvie, just hang in there. I swear to you everything is going to be fine. Trust me. I always took good care of you when we were kids, didn't I?"

"Yes, you did. But, Tom is—"

"You let *me* worry about Tom."

Their voices trailed off as they headed down the hall. Neither Dr. Augustin or I moved until we heard the elevator doors close. Then, the surge of adrenaline spent, I felt my knees buckle and, without Dr. Augustin grabbing my elbow, would have taken a closer look at the new carpeting.

"Are you all right?" he asked me, after I was safely seated in a nearby chair.

"Oh, sure," I answered. "As if breaking and entering isn't bad enough, we have to eavesdrop on a murderer." I took a couple of deep breaths and felt better. "Who was that guy? I take it you recognized his voice?"

"I've listened to that jackass bellow for too many years *not* to recognize him. It was Stanley Tohlman. *Commissioner* Stanley Tohlman. That woman, Sylvia Rheems, must be Tohlman's sister."

Dr. Augustin pulled me to my feet. He went over to the desk and quickly stuffed the magazines and the shipping schedule back in the drawer. He folded up the copy he'd made and tucked it into his back pocket. Then he steered me toward the exit.

"Let's get going," he said, "while the going is good."

CHAPTER 28

•

We didn't talk much on the way back to the clinic. I knew better than to open my mouth uninvited. Dr. Augustin's face, illuminated by the glow from the Jeep's dashboard and the occasional streetlight, was intense, turbulent. I figured he was fuming about the clown image projected by Commissioner Tohlman. Dr. Augustin was a lot of things, but buffoon certainly wasn't one of them.

"So what are you going to do?" I asked finally as Dr. Augustin unlocked the front door, and we went in. He threw the dead bolt. Lights were still on everywhere.

"Call the cops. That Detective What's-his-name wanted me to cooperate. Now I'm cooperating." He stopped in the doorway to his office and aimed his eyes at me. "We overheard Tohlman and Sylvia Rheems downstairs by the elevator."

It wasn't a suggestion. I nodded.

"I'll just hang on to this shipping schedule for future reference," he added, patting his pocket. "In case Detective . . ."

"Weller," I said.

"In case Detective Weller is too stupid to deduce the obvious."

He certainly shouldn't have any trouble deducing how you managed to acquire *that,* I thought glumly.

Dr. Augustin walked over to his desk and began punching numbers on the telephone.

I turned and headed down the hall. We still had treatments to do, murder investigation or no, and it was obvious I wasn't going to get any help from Dr. Augustin. I looked at my watch. It was 9:40.

"Feels more like midnight," I said aloud as I walked into Isolation. I was light-headed and a little queasy. I thought about the hot dogs and popcorn I hadn't eaten at the track. Then I thought about the Rose and Crown, about meat pies and frosty mugs of beer.

Suddenly something black darted across the floor and out past my leg.

"Charlie, you little snot! How did you get out?" The cat disappeared back into the kennel, and the barking grew louder by several decibels. For just the briefest moment I felt a twinge of guilt. Perhaps Frank had been telling the truth after all. I shrugged and opened the Wilkins file.

The little poodle appeared to be resting comfortably. "Maybe we can skip your pill tonight, Randy," I said to the dog. He wagged his pom-pom of a tail and lolled his tongue. It was a nice pink color.

I took the file and was on my way to Dr. Augustin's office when I heard a car drive up. Through the glass, I could see Detective Weller sitting behind the wheel. He'd turned off the engine, but hadn't gotten out yet. His hands were still on the steering wheel, and he was staring at my car.

"Your buddy Weller is here," I said into Dr. Augustin's office. "By the way, do you want to continue medicating the Wilkins dog? His color is really good, and his breathing is almost normal."

"No, we'll see how he looks in the morning."

I went back to Isolation and, after making a few notes in the Wilkins record, opened up the next file.

I didn't hear Dr. Augustin unlock the front door. The barking from the kennel was too loud. And I missed whatever the two of them said to each other when Detective Weller first stepped into the reception room. I figured it must have been five or six minutes from the time I announced the detective's arrival until I heard Dr. Augustin shout.

"What the hell . . . ?"

"Don't fuck with me, mister." It was Weller's voice all right, but it hadn't come from the same Weller I'd spoken to earlier that month. *This* Weller meant business. I started for the hall.

"I'm not 'fucking' with you," Dr. Augustin said, a little too loudly. "I swear to God, there's no one else here. I had to take Samantha home. Her car wouldn't start." He made a stab at laughter. "That's the third time this week."

I backed into the row of cages along the north wall and held my breath.

"Listen, we can talk about this, can't we? You don't need that gun. I'm not going to cause you any trouble."

"You and your ex-wife have already caused us more trouble than you know. Stan was right. We should have gotten rid of that woman back in November. Now we'll have to get rid of you both."

I could see the hall telephone. It was a tantalizing six feet away. Of course, using it meant Weller would spot me if he happened to look that way. Then I remembered the extension in the kennel. All I had to do was slip into the surgery and dash across the hall. The kennel door had to be open. Otherwise, how had Charlie gotten out?

I ran through the connecting doorway into Surgery and

looked into the kennel. Charlie was on the shelf with the food dishes. He'd ripped a small hole in a bag of dry dog food and was helping himself. He looked over at me, his eyes like tiny luminescent orbs. He grabbed one last mouthful, hopped to the floor, and disappeared again.

I took several deep breaths, then peeked cautiously around the corner. Detective Weller had his back to me, but I could see he had a gun pointed at Dr. Augustin. I plunged across the hall. I wasn't sure if Dr. Augustin had seen me, but I prayed he wouldn't react. I grabbed the phone and punched 911, fully expecting to get an automated voice telling me to please wait.

"What is your emergency?" a pleasant-sounding woman asked me.

"This is Samantha Holt, Paradise Cay Animal Hospital," I said very quickly and softly. "We are being robbed, and the man has a gun. I think he plans to use it. Please hurry."

Before she could respond, I heard a rattle behind me. I jumped and turned around, dropping the receiver. It swung wildly on its cord, crashing against the wall several times before coming to a rest. I ignored it, mesmerized by the scene playing out in front of me.

Charlie was standing on his hind legs against the door to Mad Max's cage. Like he'd done it a million times before, he reached up with his right paw and pushed on the latch. The door popped open. Charlie immediately ran over to the counter by the sink and jumped up. As if on cue, two hundred pounds of fawn-colored muscle and drool exploded from the run and headed for the kennel door. Once in the hallway, Max lost his footing for a second, and his nails ratcheted wildly on the flooring. He soon got it together and took off again for the reception room.

I couldn't look. I waited for the shot, but instead heard a

cry of surprise, followed by a loud thud. I risked a glance in the direction of the sound and saw Max standing on Detective Weller's chest. Dr. Augustin reached down and took the gun out of Weller's hand, then attempted to pull Max away. I grabbed a leash off the peg by the door and went to help. We finally succeeded in dragging Max over to Cynthia's desk.

Through it all, Dr. Augustin kept the gun pointed more or less at Weller's head, but it was an unnecessary precaution. The detective was out cold.

CHAPTER 29

•

Friday, March 4

The day started out pretty close to normal. Dr. Augustin was in a rotten mood. It wound up being our word against Detective Weller's, regarding how he came to be unconscious on our reception-room floor. Dr. Augustin, of course, told the patrolmen what *really* happened, but you certainly couldn't expect them to doubt one of their own. Weller threatened to sue, and Dr. Augustin nearly punched the detective in the mouth.

After the ambulance took Detective Weller off to the hospital for observation, one of the patrolmen halfheartedly said he'd "look into it," presumably meaning he'd file a report about what we "allegedly" overheard at the track, and that would be that.

"What if Weller and good ol' Commissioner Tohlman really *do* decide to 'get rid of us'?" I asked Dr. Augustin during morning treatments. "Like Weller threatened to do? What if—"

"Calm *down*, Samantha," he snapped. "They wouldn't dare risk it. Not now. Not after last night's ruckus and our 'alleged' eavesdropping. If I were Tohlman, I'd lay low until I was sure the cops had bought Weller's story. He wouldn't have to get rid of us then."

"But what are you going to do if the cops don't

investigate Tohlman? What if they don't check out Bayside? What are you going to do *then,* to get Rachel out of jail?"

"I guess I'll have to pay Mr. Toureau another visit. Maybe help myself to a few 'sample products.'"

I gulped audibly. If that was the case, what was to keep Dr. Augustin, or me for that matter, from having a little accident one evening on the way home?

Dr. Augustin started for his office, but stopped and turned around. "Have Frank put a padlock on Charlie's cage. I'm grateful for what that cat did, but we can't have our 'guests' roaming the halls at night, now, can we?" He didn't wait for me to answer.

At 11:30, Michael stopped by. I was in the storeroom behind the reception desk, checking our supply of dog food, when I heard Cynthia squeal with delight.

"Oh, Mike, it's so good to see you! Come over here and give me a hug."

I waited a few seconds, then stepped out, smiling. I had to admit, it *was* nice to get a visit from someone not directly involved in our "case."

"Hi," I said.

"Hi, yourself," he answered. He was wearing his yachting ensemble—polo shirt, tan slacks, expensive deck shoes, no socks. All he needed was a hat and some zinc oxide on his nose. "Listen, is there a quiet place we can talk? I have some interesting news I think you and Dr. Augustin will want to hear."

"Sure. I guess so." I tapped lightly on Dr. Augustin's door, then opened it a crack. "Michael wants to talk to us," I said.

Dr. Augustin nodded and pointed to the chair next to his desk, but he never looked up from the book he was reading. That might indicate enthusiasm, I thought. Heaven forbid.

I showed Michael in and closed the door behind us. He walked over to the chair and sat down. I continued to stand.

"Greetings, Dr. Augustin. Interesting evening you had yesterday."

Dr. Augustin put down his book and glared at me.

"Oh, don't blame Samantha," Michael said. "I read all about it in Officer Whitfield's report. It seems that Bayside Meats has been processing more than just dog food these last few months." He was smiling broadly.

Dr. Augustin stared at him, then leaned forward. His expression was mixed. Anticipation, suspicion. Lines and creases I'd never noticed before made him look older.

"The police got a search warrant for Tohlman's house," Michael continued, "and apparently found an undisclosed amount of cocaine, several thousand dollars in cash, and evidence our esteemed commissioner had a hand in Bradley Donovan's death." He paused. "Detective Weller, an undercover detective working out of the Narcotics Division, opened up like a ripe watermelon. Implicated Tohlman, Rheems, the Toureau brothers. Said Donovan acted as a go-between there at the track." He seemed to be waiting for some kind of response from Dr. Augustin. When he didn't get any, he went on. "I'm told the DEA raided Bayside Meats early this morning, but I don't have any of the details. So far, it looks like Stellar Enterprises is off the hook. Again."

Dr. Augustin crossed his arms and slouched back in his chair. I noticed he had brightened considerably. "So, I take it they were using the track to distribute the drugs."

Michael shook his head. "Actually, according to Weller, none of the stuff was being peddled out at the track. Too many state pari-mutuel people. They sold it mostly through neighborhood dealers. Lots of small-time distribution. It added up to a lot of money, though." He winked at me, and I felt myself blush.

Dr. Augustin never noticed. He was too caught up in the moment. "Stanley Tohlman has been a commissioner here for six years," he said. "I presume Bayside Meats only started this smuggling operation last year, when Toureau bought the place. Was Tohlman involved with someone else before that?"

Michael shook his head. "According to Weller, Tohlman was recruited last year by Stellar Enterprises, when they were looking to set up shop here in the Tampa Bay area. Tohlman has a gambling problem, apparently. Sporting events like baseball and football, as well as the puppies. He owes a lot of money to a lot of people and was an easy target.

"He got his brother-in-law, an accountant in Chicago, to move down here and apply for the kennel club's assistant-manager position. Then he made sure he got it. Political clout, I guess. The track needed a permit for some major renovations to its restaurant."

Dr. Augustin stood up and stretched. The lines and furrows were nearly gone.

"Does this mean they'll let Rachel go?" I asked.

"Undoubtedly," Michael said. "Probably sometime this afternoon. I'll head on over to the jail and check it out, if you like." He stood.

Dr. Augustin put a hand on Michael's shoulder. "We'd appreciate that." He smiled. "I'm not going to ask you how you found out about Tohlman and Weller so quickly. But I am grateful." He stuck out his hand.

Michael shook it. "Glad to help," he said, then he winked at me again.

This time Dr. Augustin noticed. He made a point of rolling his eyes.

EPILOGUE

•

Two men from the DEA office in Tampa came by at three to question us. Of course, by that time they already knew more than we did. The building within a building at Bayside Meats was an efficient little laboratory, where Toureau and company turned cocaine into crack. Pretty slick operation. I think Dr. Augustin expected the feds to thank him for leading them to Toureau, but they disappointed him.

Rachel was released sometime around four. I overheard Dr. Augustin talking to her on the phone. I hadn't meant to eavesdrop, but I couldn't help myself.

He asked her if she'd like to have dinner with him, to celebrate. Apparently, she had other plans. He sat at his desk for a while after hanging up. Then he came out to the reception room. His face was clear, almost tranquil, if that was possible.

"I thought you had a date with Michael," he said. He looked at his watch. "It's nearly six." That was the first time he'd used Michael Halsey's first name. I hadn't imagined it.

"I told him I didn't feel well," I said. "That I was too tired. You know . . . after everything that's happened." I began moving things around on the reception desk, pretending to clean it. Suddenly I couldn't look at him.

He leaned against the wall next to me. I could smell his bubble gum. "How do you feel now?"

"Okay, I guess," I said, shuffling papers about. Cynthia is going to kill me, I thought.

"Rachel called," he said.

"Oh?"

"They found Blue Moon. She and Paul Connelly. Wandering around over near the farm."

"That's great news," I said.

"Yeah, it is, isn't it?"

I looked up. He was grinning.

"Want to split a pitcher at the Rose and Crown?" he asked.

Afraid I might appear too eager, I didn't answer him right away. He didn't move.

"You buying?"

"I thought maybe you'd like to buy. That bet you made last night paid off. Domino Joe came in first. You won twenty-four bucks."

"Hey, no kidding? Sure. I'll buy."

"No," he said, "that's okay. It'll be my treat." He was smirking. "But we need to get there before happy hour is over. Two for one is the only way I'll be able to afford you, the way you drink."

I wadded up a piece of paper and threw it at him. "Then we'd better hurry," I said.